BLINK DREAD

SPIKE BLACK

Published by High Concept Books

ISBN: 9781520286815

For D.A.W.N.

CHAPTER 1

I blink hard and rub my eyes. It's been a long day and I didn't sleep well last night. Or even at all... It's sometimes hard to tell when pockets of sleep steal you away to unconsciousness. I blink again, my vision settling into focus just as the dump truck ahead of me rolls on. I depress the accelerator and edge forward.

"Come on, come *on*..."

A quick glance at the dashboard clock. *15:33.* My stomach twists.

The truck pulls level with the junction.

"Okay. Okay, let's go."

I step on the gas just as the stoplight changes to red.

"No! Damn it, you son of a bitch!"

Punching the center of the steering wheel, I blast the horn in error, inadvertently rousing the frustration of my fellow commuters, whose vehicles proceed to fill the air with an orchestra of beeps and honks.

Dropping back into the seat, a growl escapes my lips. It's hard not to believe that the world is somehow conspiring against me, that all the traffic lights I've passed since leaving the factory are working in perfect synchronicity in an effort to make me late.

The smell of exhaust fumes rattles my sinuses. The truck's bumper sticker reads: *MIND IF I SMOKE?* Somewhere in the back of my mind I find that amusing.

The cramped interior of my old Ford Fiesta is a mess. With one eye on the road, I empty the ashtray out of the side window and clear the passenger seat of sci-fi magazines and old food cartons, throwing them out of sight in the back. I can't have Mia reporting bad things to her mother. It's important I give the impression that things are going well for me.

Across the junction, the spire of Chalkstone Primary School's clock tower rises above the other Victorian red brick buildings, taunting me. Most of the other children will have been handed off to their parents by now. I imagine Mia scanning the playground for me, perhaps getting a little tearful.

The clock's display flicks to *15:35*.

The stoplight is still red.

If I'm not there in the next five minutes, Mia's teacher is going to pick up the phone and call my wife, because hers is the designated emergency contact number, and all of my hard work these past three years to persuade Hazel to change her mind about me will have been for nothing. Because if I can't even pick up our daughter from school on time, then what use am I?

At last, the lights change and the traffic surges forward. I'm across the junction in moments, the school in the next street along. I can still make it. I'm in a residential area with cars lining both sides of the road, though, so I need to watch my speed.

I can't wait to see her, even if it's just for a couple of hours before bedtime. We'll have dinner on our laps in front of *Mickey Mouse Clubhouse*. I'll read her a story or two.

A man darts out from between two parked cars.

"Christ, no…"

I slam on the brakes, bracing myself. The car jerks to a halt. I lunge forward, the seat belt pulling tight and knocking the air from my lungs in a sharp, gasping breath.

My head snaps up, desperate eyes scanning the road ahead.

Thank God.

The man stands there, eyes wide with alarm, staring in at me. The car's bumper has come to a stop less than two feet from where he's standing, and yet it appears he made no effort to get out of the road as I bore down on him. His attire offers a clue to his state of mind: a pair of heavily-creased, blue-and-white striped pajamas. In the middle of the afternoon.

My mind makes an instant connection with my late grandfather, who would often slip unnoticed from his residential home and go for a wander in his nightclothes. Except that the guy standing in the road isn't old at all. Late twenties, perhaps. Certainly no older than me.

And he's mouthing something.

Unclipping the seat belt, I push open the door and leap out.

The man is barefoot. His eyes continue staring, almost obscenely wide. He's in a state of shock, I guess.

"Hospital," the man says.

I'm speechless for a moment. Does he think I'm running a taxi service, here?

"What the hell...?" I splutter. "What are you doing? Are you trying to get yourself killed?"

"Hospital," the man repeats. "Please."

It's clear now, face to face with the guy, that there's something seriously wrong with him. My fury dissipates in an instant.

His panicked eyes bulge like marbles from sunken sockets. "King's Hill. Please, you've got to help me."

There's a horrible desperation in his voice, as if he'll drop dead at any moment if I don't do something.

"I'll call an ambulance," I say, pulling out my phone.

"No!" the man screams. "No time. We have to go now!"

He moves sideways in a crab-like fashion around the front of my car, away from me.

"Hey!" I know exactly what he's doing. I chase after him.

The man pulls open the passenger door.

Son of a bitch. I close on him.

The man's arms fly up. "Don't touch me! Don't fucking touch me!"

I stop dead. Take a step back, raising my palms. "Okay, okay."

Shit. The guy's a madman. What the hell have I got myself into, here?

He slides into the passenger seat and closes the door.

I run around to the driver's side and climb in. A horn blasts. Someone's behind me now.

I'm in such a panic that I've forgotten how to drive.

I fumble with the controls. The car feels cramped with the two of us side by side. A musty smell emanates from the guy, as if he's worn those pajamas for far too long.

My heart hammers in my chest, the rush of adrenalin causing my hands to tremble. I pause for breath. Sliding the car into gear, I almost hit the man's knee.

"Watch it!" he shouts, moving his leg away. "Do not touch me!"

Yeah, yeah. I get it.

I pull away. Take a moment to gather myself. "So what's wrong with you?" I ask. A little forward, perhaps, but I figure I've earned the right to know. Besides, I want the assurance that this will all be worth it.

"Just drive," the man says.

A real charmer, this guy.

"And no loud noises."

I glance over to check if he's pulling my leg. "What?"

"You know, if you can help it. And keep the sudden movements to a minimum."

It occurs to me that this whole thing could be some kind of elaborate wind-up.

My passenger glares back, deadly serious, the whites of his eyes visible around the entire perimeter of the iris. I know that look, and it strikes fear into my heart. The very last thing I need right now is for Hazel to find out that I've had a junkie in my car.

I turn right at the end of the road. Chalkstone Primary is up ahead on the left. There's no way I can collect Mia now, not with a crazed drug addict riding shotgun. I drive on past without even looking over. I don't want her to see me if she's standing in the doorway.

"Can't this thing go any faster?" my passenger says.

"You know, there's a medical center at the back of the rec. If I take the next turning we'll be there in, like…"

"No. It has to be King's Hill."

Great. King's Hill is forty minutes away. But the guy is of such sickly appearance that I don't feel able to argue with him. The deathly pallor of his skin accentuates the purple bags underscoring his wild eyes. Drops of sweat collect in his unkempt eyebrows.

It feels uncomfortable having a stranger in the car with me, and I can't stand the silence. I reach forward to turn the dial on the radio, and then remember what he said about sudden loud noises. I sit back again. "I'm Ajay, by the way."

The guy stares ahead, breathing heavy. "Zack."

More silence. I continue along the bleak, factory-laden streets, heading out of town.

Just as I'm thinking the guy won't speak again for the rest of the journey, Zack says, "Listen, thanks for picking me up."

Yeah, because you really gave me a choice in the matter.

"No worries."

"Sorry if I scared you," Zack says, his voice shaking. "I know I must look like a freak."

Glancing over, I take a moment to study him. His hands tremble involuntarily in his lap. A frosting of stubble decorates the lower half of his narrow face. His eyelids twitch as they hang precariously over bloodshot eyes.

"Well, if I'm honest, you do look like you need a good night's sleep."

Zack's face hardens. "You mustn't let me sleep. Do you understand?"

Ugh. Whatever.

I want to say it out loud, but I'm too much of a coward and nod instead. *Jesus.* I should have just driven around him in the road and kept on going.

As I follow signs to the motorway, I realize that there's something else really bothering me about this guy. Something oddly more disturbing than his deathly appearance or the afternoon pajamas or his seriously unhinged demeanor.

Zack hasn't blinked once.

CHAPTER 2

I watch in the rearview mirror as Chalkstone Primary's clock tower fades into the distance. Feeling Zack's eyes burning into me, I turn my head and, sure enough, he's staring back, his permanently shocked expression all the more disconcerting when accompanied by complete silence.

"What?"

"Nothing," he says, continuing to stare anyway.

I blink, hoping to encourage him to do the same, but Zack's gaze remains unbroken. I return my attention to the road ahead. Okay, so I appreciate that there's something wrong with the guy, and that perhaps he can't help it, but still—that unrelenting stare makes my guts churn. The sooner we reach King's Hill, the better.

Taking the phone from my pocket, I slide it into the hands-free dock mounted to the dashboard and swipe down the list of contacts. I stop at one name, *The Dragon*, and after a brief moment of hesitation, tap the screen.

Calling The Dragon, the phone informs me.

A woman's voice comes through the speaker. "Hello?"

"Brenda, it's Ajay. I'm so sorry, but I need you to do me a massive favor."

There's an agonizing pause. "You didn't collect her, did you?"

"I was on my way, I swear, but something came up."

"Came *up*?"

"An emergency. I'm sorry to have to do this, but do you think—"

She sighs. "I'm just getting my coat."

"Thank you. I'm really grateful."

"This isn't the way to go if you want to keep seeing her, you know."

"Absolutely, I appreciate that. It'll just be this one time…"

"How long?"

"Sorry?"

"How long will you be?"

"Oh. I'm not sure. A couple of hours, maybe?"

A door slams in the background. At least I know she's on her way.

"I knew this would happen," she says, the line crackling as the wind hits her phone. "I just knew it. I told Hazel, I told her never to trust you again, and now look."

"I'm sorry, I—"

"I've been around the block, see. I know your type. But she just had to give you a second chance. She's too forgiving, that girl."

I'm suddenly painfully aware that Zack can hear every word. "Well anyway, thanks for doing this. I'll be there as soon as I can." Brenda starts speaking again, but I cut in. "I appreciate it. Bye." I end the call with a jab of my finger.

"Christ, I'm sorry," Zack says after a moment. "I totally messed up your plans."

I look over and, to my surprise, Zack seems genuinely remorseful. Maybe I judged the guy too harshly. "No, no, it's fine. Not your fault." Or is it? What do I know about this guy and his problems? Maybe it's all self-inflicted. "I'm glad I could help. Lucky I was passing by, really."

I traverse the roundabout at the edge of town, silver birch trees rushing past on both sides as the road carves a path through the flat Suffolk countryside.

"So," Zack says. "You got a kid?"

"Yeah. She's just turned five. You?"

"Oh, no, no. Thank goodness. I wouldn't want them…" He trails off.

I glance over, wanting him to continue, but Zack avoids my gaze.

"Are you married, then?" he asks.

I snort. "Well, technically. She works at King's Hill, as it happens."

"Oh yeah?"

"Yes. She's an oncology nurse."

Zack stares at me blankly.

"On the cancer ward."

"Yes, yes," he says impatiently. "I know what oncology means."

I grimace. With this guy, a blank stare is not an indicator that he doesn't understand something. It's just par for the course.

After two more roundabouts, I navigate the slip road and filter onto the motorway. The rush hour traffic is mostly in the opposite lane coming away from the city, so we should have a clear run. Thank goodness.

"I was doing a clinical trial," Zack says. "At King's Hill."

I shoot him a look. "Sorry?"

"You asked what's wrong with me."

"Oh. Right."

"You know what a pilot study is?"

I shake my head.

"Well, this one was testing a potential cure for dry eye disease. They injected us into our eyeballs."

I wince. That has to be the worst combination of words anyone has ever uttered. "They did *what?*"

"It's not as bad as it sounds. They give you anesthetic."

"Still, I mean... *ugh*. That's just..." I blink hard. My eyeballs ache in empathy. "I just couldn't do that. Oh, man..."

"We spent three nights under observation, quarantined in the ward. But the deal was you had to stay awake. If you fell asleep even once, you didn't get paid. But it was cool. We were being paid to play video games, pretty much."

"Wow." I'm genuinely impressed. Why have I never thought about doing clinical trials? Oh yeah, that's why. Because they do things like *inject needles directly into your eyeballs.*

"Cool, huh?" Zack says. "They even had some new releases, like *Medieval Dead 4*."

"You're kidding?"

"No. What?"

"That's not even out yet."

"Huh?"

"Oh, yeah." If there's one thing I know a lot about, it's zombie video games. They are, after all, partly responsible for the failure of my marriage.

"Twenty-sixth of June next year, that's the official release date."

Zack sighs heavily.

I glance over. It's difficult to gauge the guy's emotions with those scary eyes glaring at me.

"You calling me a liar?" he says.

"What? No, no. They just had an early release copy or something, that's all. Games companies do that sometimes." *Good God.* It's like walking on eggshells with this guy.

He dismisses me with a wave of the hand. "Whatever. So anyway, I got through it. I completed the trial this morning. Of course, as soon as I got home, I went straight to bed. I was more tired than I've ever felt in my life…"

It barely shows in your temperament at all, I want to say, and stifle a laugh. "I should imagine you were."

"But that's just it," Zack says. He's getting increasingly agitated. "I couldn't sleep. Every time I tried there was… there was this *thing*. A white dot in the center of my vision, right there when I closed my eyes."

"Yeah, I get that sometimes. It's the start of a migraine. Probably due to lack of sleep."

"That's what I thought, too. At first, anyway. But then I started seeing it every time I blinked. And the more I blinked, the larger it got, until…"

I wait for him to continue, but Zack has stopped talking. "Until what?"

"Anyway, that's when Doctor Roman called—this is the guy doing the trial—and he said that I had to get back to King's Hill immediately. To get there as soon as I could, by whatever means necessary. Because I was infected with something."

A ball of terror forms in the pit of my stomach. "Jesus Christ, what?"

"I don't know. He's found an antidote, so as long as I get there in time, he'll sort me out. But he said that I absolutely must not close my eyes, or even touch anyone, because this thing…" His voice catches in his throat.

I shrink away from him instinctively. "What? For God's sake, what?"

Zack turns to face me, his eyes bulging in an unsightly fashion, his mouth opening ready to speak.

A creepy tune fills the silence. I freeze in horror, goosebumps rippling the flesh on my arms.

I recognize the blast of music and relax. It's the opening theme tune from *The Twilight Zone*. I've set it as my ringtone for whenever Hazel calls. "Well?"

Zack stares at the flashing phone. "Shouldn't you get that?"

I deflate. I should, yes, but my heart is hammering so hard in my chest that I don't think I can deal with her right now.

The guy's full of crap, a voice in my head assures me. *A bullshit artist. It's probably the drugs talking. Don't listen to him.*

I tap the screen to answer the call.

The sound of my wife's voice fills the car. "What the hell, Ajay?"

"Yeah, look, I'm really sorry, okay? I—"

"Sorry won't cut it, don't you understand?"

"I know, I know, but something came up."

"Really? Something more important than your daughter?"

My passenger's head drops. "It's my fault," Zack says. "I'm so sorry."

"Who's that?" Hazel demands.

I cringe. "Nobody. Don't worry. Just someone I picked up."

"Was that Trevor?"

"What? No…"

"Are you hanging with your buddies? Is that what this is?"

"No, no. Listen, I'll be there soon, okay?"

"You picked up one of your mates instead of your daughter?"

"Look, there's been an emergency. I'm coming to the hospital."

"Why? Did Trevor OD again or something?"

I switch to the outside lane of the motorway and increase my speed. "It's not like that anymore, okay? And it's not Trevor. It's just... it's just some bloke I found in the road."

"Thanks," Zack says.

"Listen, Hazel, we're on our way now. I don't know—maybe I'll see you there."

There's a pause on the end of the line. "I'm on the ward, Ajay."

"We'll have a coffee or something. On your break."

"Oh, Jesus. Don't you get it? You've got to get back to pick up Mia. You can't just put this all on my mother."

"You're right, of course. I'm sorry. I just wanted to see you, that's all."

I wait. Silence on Hazel's end.

Maybe she's hung up. "Hello?"

She sighs. "Why?"

"Well, you know..."

"It's over, okay?"

"Yeah, but..."

"It's over."

I don't know what else to say, but I have to try something. My mind races through possible responses, but before I can formulate anything Hazel's voice comes over the speaker.

"I'm seeing someone."

My face flushes hot. My stomach somersaults. I think I might vomit over the steering wheel. "I'm sorry, what?"

"He's a doctor."

It takes a few heartbeats for me to process this information. "At King's Hill?"

"I'm moving on, okay? We both are. Mia can't be around a pot head like you."

I raise a hand to the heavens. "For goodness sake, Hazel, how many times? It's not like that anymore. You can trust me."

"Right, right. Like I trusted you to pick up Mia."

"You know I'm clean. Have been for three years now. And I've got a job."

She scoffs. "For how long? You've never kept a job for, what? More than six months?"

I notice that I'm driving ten miles over the speed limit and ease off on the accelerator. "I'll pick her up soon, okay?"

"You had to do one thing, Ajay. One thing. And you can't even do that. You'll lose all custody, you know that, don't you? Is that what you want?"

"Of course not."

"Look, I'm really busy here. I've got to go."

"Okay, hang on—"

The call ends.

I blink. Stare at the road ahead, driving steady. My mind is numb.

Dark shadows stretch across the carriageway as the sun lowers over the fields.

A doctor. Man, how am I ever going to compete with that?

"Anyway," I say, suddenly needing the distraction of Zack's bullshit. "Carry on. What were you saying?"

He doesn't respond.

"Please, I want to know. I'm—"

The words lodge in my throat as I glance over and see something that strikes fear into my heart.

Zack is asleep.

CHAPTER 3

"Zack! Come on, wake up! Zack!"

He doesn't stir.

I consider leaving him alone. The guy has, after all, been craving sleep for the past three days and has at last succumbed. That is, of course, if he's been telling the truth. And given the physical evidence of his tiredness, I'm inclined to think that he has.

"Zack!"

A good sleep never hurt anybody though, right? And he certainly doesn't appear to be in any danger, curled up on the seat with his head leaning to one side, a thin runner of dribble hanging from the corner of his downturned mouth.

It also means that I don't have to keep looking into those goddamned *eyes*.

But Zack absolutely insisted that I not let him sleep. And what if he's right? What if something terrible really *is* going to happen to him if he closes his eyes for a sustained period of time?

Granted, it's more likely that Zack is just some paranoid nutcase who fears that the men in white coats are going to come for him while he sleeps. Or maybe he has some kind of mental condition that makes him think sleep is in some way harmful to his health.

But whether what he believes is true or not, it doesn't change the fact that he won't be too pleased, when he does eventually wake up, to discover that I've left him to sleep it off. And if the guy is even half as unstable as I suspect, then there's no telling what he's capable of doing to me in the throes of some kind of psychotic rage...

"Zack! Hey, wake up! Come on! Zack!"

No response.

He's too far gone, too deep in sleep.

Or dead already.

"Oh, crap!" I veer over to the inside lane, the tires screaming as I pump the brake pedal. Navigating onto the shoulder, I pull up the handbrake and lean over, shaking Zack by the shoulders.

"Hey, pal. Wake up!"

I examine his face for signs of life. He has an eyebrow piercing that I never noticed before.

Vehicles thunder past on the main carriageway. I hold my breath. Start to wonder what the course of action is when you have a dead body in your car.

Zack jerks awake with a gasp, his eyes red and momentarily glazed. "Huh?"

Then reality hits and he cries out, snapping into an upright position. Eyes wide, mouth open, his breath a series of panting gasps.

"Zack? Are—"

"No!" he yells. "No, Jesus, no!"

"What is it? What's wrong?"

"If I fall asleep I'm dead!"

"Well... you look okay to me."

"You don't understand," he says, the words struggling to come as he pants and swallows, his mouth unable to fully form the words in his state of rigid panic. "This thing..."

He stares into the middle distance, his face a mask of undiluted terror.

"Stay with me, Zack. You're okay. You're doing fine."

"This *creature*..."

His breath quickens dramatically, to the point that I'm convinced he's going to hyperventilate. Then, suddenly, he grips tight to the sides of the chair, as if bracing himself, and closes his eyes.

They fly open a second later. "Oh, God. It's right on me!"

"What? What are you talking about?"

"One more blink and I'm done for. Oh no!" He dissolves into a crying fit, sobs choking in his throat, his eyes remaining wide open the entire time, drilling into me, pleading with me to do something. "Oh my God, oh my God!"

I look on in utter helplessness. "Zack?"

"Hospital."

"What?"

"King's Hill. Just go, go!"

I burst into action, throwing the car into gear, removing the handbrake and pulling off the shoulder, almost killing us both as a tanker truck hurtles past, horn blaring. I stamp on the brake.

"Gah!" Zack cries as he jerks forward.

I fully understand now why sudden movements are not a good idea in Zack's condition.

I study the lane in the rearview mirror. The wait to rejoin the flow of traffic, with Zack moaning in terror beside me, is excruciating. My teeth grind together in impatience. I grip the steering wheel hard to steady my trembling hands.

With a gap opening up, I pull away safely, then glance over to make sure that Zack's okay.

Tears stream down his pale, elongated face. "There's nothing can be done," he says. "It's too late now. I'm finished."

"Nonsense." I'm trying hard to sound upbeat. "We're only a few miles away."

"It doesn't matter. We won't get there in time."

"Oh no?" I sail across to the overtaking lane and put my foot down.

"I just know," Zack says. "I can't hold out. I just can't."

The speedometer needle rises past ninety. Ninety-five. "Sure you can."

"No. There's only one thing for it."

I'm so busy trying to maintain control of the car at this speed that I daren't look over. From the corner of my vision I see Zack taking something from the pocket of his pajama pants.

I ease off the accelerator and glance across.

A box cutter.

Zack extends the blade and puts it to his eye.

"What are you doing?" My voice is a high-pitched whine.

"Better this than dead," Zack says. He holds his upper right eyelid between the thumb and forefinger of his left hand and presses down on the blade. The knife slices into the corner of his eyelid.

"Oh, Jesus!" My stomach turns. "Stop that, for God's sake!"

Zack continues on, grimacing as the blade carves through flesh.

"Please…" The car's speed drops dramatically. "I have an eye thing, remember?"

Blood trickles down the side of Zack's face, his hand mercifully obscuring my view of his eye, the knife blade glinting as it reflects the glow of the late afternoon sun.

An upcoming motorway sign announces: ELDHAM 7 MILES.

"Look!" I point frantically at the sign. "We're almost there!"

Zack pauses for a moment, then exhales. He drops the knife into his lap and turns to me.

I fight the impulse to gag. Zack's upper eyelid is now mangled and flapping unnaturally, the damaged nerve endings causing it to flutter like some kind of grotesque, blood-soaked butterfly.

"O-kay," I say. "That's…that's good." Maybe finishing the job would have been a better idea, after all. "This doctor, he's got the cure, right?"

Zack nods.

"Right. Well, then we just have to get you there."

He sighs heavily, his breath shaking. He presses a lever on the side of the box cutter and the bloodied blade retracts into the handle.

"That's better," I say, struggling to get my breath back. "Not far now, okay?"

I steadily increase my speed once more. From the corner of my eye I can see that Zack still holds a tight grip on the knife. What is this psycho going to do next? Stab me as I drive? Maybe, if I don't drive fast enough, he will.

Thinking of Mia, and of getting back to her, I steel to the task at hand. I press the gas pedal to the floor and send us hurtling toward our destination.

CHAPTER 4

I whip into a disabled bay outside King's Hill hospital's main entrance and leap out. Grabbing a wheelchair parked beside the revolving doors, I steer it to the passenger side of the car.

Zack opens the door and swings his legs out. "Don't touch me!" he yells, holding up his hands.

"Here," I say. "Get in. Just concentrate on keeping your eyes open."

He glares at me with contempt before hopping into the chair. I know not to take it personally—that's his default facial expression, after all.

I wheel him up the slope, through the large revolving doors and into the lobby, a wide space with a high ceiling and gentle lighting. Vast canvases of lush tropical landscapes decorate the walls.

Everything is business as usual: a line of visitors at the information desk, a flurry of patients and staff passing through. Nearby, a middle-aged bald woman in a white gown argues with a security guard about the hospital's no-smoking policy.

I grab the attention of an orderly. He comes over.

"Doctor Roman," Zack says to him. "Clinical Research Ward. Pronto."

The orderly takes the wheelchair from me and pushes Zack across the lobby.

"See you, then," I say. I expect no gratitude from him, and receive none. All the same, I wish him well. Zack is a very troubled individual.

"Wait!" Zack cries out, holding his hand up. The orderly stops.

Zack peers over his shoulder, meeting my eye. "Did you touch me?"

"What?" I can't believe this guy. "No, I didn't bloody well touch you."

He spins the chair around to face me. "No, I mean back in the car, when you woke me up. Did you touch me?"

I think back: I pulled over onto the shoulder. Checked for signs that Zack was still alive.

Shook him.

"Well, yeah. I mean, you'd fallen asleep. I had to do something."

"Okay, I have some bad news." Zack exhales. "Now you've got it, too."

I swallow. Can't speak for a moment. "Got what?"

"You need to see Roman."

"No, no, I'm going. I've got to pick up my daughter, remember?"

"Trust me, you do not want to pass this onto her." He places a hand in the pocket of his pajama pants. "You'll need this." He rummages around, trying to find something.

I know what he's searching for. "Wait—no. Just stop. I don't need it."

"Well, then don't close your eyes. Don't fall asleep. Don't even blink."

He signals to the orderly, who turns the chair around and wheels him away, through a set of double doors.

"Why?" I call after him. "What is it? What is this thing?"

Just as the doors are about to shut, Zack yells out. "You'll see."

CHAPTER 5

People mill around me as, rooted to the spot, I stare at the door Zack has just disappeared through.

You'll see. What the hell did he mean by that?

I'm too afraid to close my eyes and find out.

My eyelids are immediately heavy, my eyes irritable and in desperate need of the moisture provided by blinking.

Zack's a nutjob! Don't listen to him!

That's sensible advice. And yet, I can't bring myself to actually blink.

I turn to leave, then stop. Maybe I should get checked out, at least. I join the line at the reception desk. I've never held my eyes open for longer than necessary before, nor been conscious of my own rate of blinking. How long can I keep this up before I do some kind of lasting damage?

The line moves along, and I edge forward. *Wait*—which department do I need? And what do I say is wrong with me when I get there? Should I just go straight to the Clinical Research Ward?

I drop out of the line, tendrils of panic climbing up my insides. I wander into the middle of the lobby floor. My eyes are stinging now. There's only one thing for it.

Balling my hands into fists, I take a deep breath and close my eyes.

Nothing.

I open them, then close them again, tightly this time. I see stars, little dots of color, but that's normal when I screw my eyes shut.

When I reopen them, a passing security guard regards me suspiciously. I smile weakly and move on.

Okay. So whatever Zack has, I don't have it. Thank God. I blink a few times just because I can.

When I turn back to check, the security guard is still watching me.

I need to get out of here. On impulse, I move into the main corridor and scan the walls for signs. I know where oncology is situated, have been there a few times when meeting Hazel at the end of her shift, but my mind is so frazzled that I no longer trust my own memory or sense of direction.

The smell of disinfectant in the corridor mixed with the far-off odor of hospital food brings sudden flashes of the bad times: breaking my leg when I was ten, Nanna screaming on the ward shortly before she died, my mother's cancer. I put this jumble of thoughts and images out of my mind and press on.

I arrive at oncology more by luck than judgment, and then realize I'm not really sure why I'm here. I just want to see her, I suppose. But in order to do that, I'll have to ring the bell to gain entry to the ward, and then I'll have to explain who I am to the receptionist...

Ugh. What am I doing? This is the worst idea in the world. I'll only end up having another argument with her. And if I'd known I was coming I would have changed out of my work clothes at the end of my shift. I really don't want her to see me like this, in grotty, ill-fitting jeans and a shapeless sweatshirt ingrained with wood chippings.

I have to leave.

Sudden movement grabs my attention and I watch through the glass as a nurse in a blue-and-white striped uniform approaches the front desk. It's Hazel. My pulse quickens.

She glances my way and I gasp, stepping back. She doesn't seem to have noticed me, thank goodness.

She leans against the desk, flipping through a patient's chart. She looks good, even in her unflattering trousers and tunic combo. Really good, in fact.

My eyes inexplicably fill with tears and I blink them away. As my vision clears I see a man in pink scrubs approaching her. He's tall, bespectacled, handsome.

He presses into Hazel from behind and brushes her hip.

She turns sharply, and then relaxes into his arms. She looks around before leaning in and kissing him firmly on the lips.

I turn and start walking. Nothing is quite in focus, and I'm dizzy. I pass a young boy with eyes as wide as saucers. Moments later I'm back in the lobby, marching to the exit. A middle-aged woman collapses nearby. Two security guards rush to her aid. I assume she's having some kind of fit, and leave them to it.

I'm outside the hospital building, by the side of my car, with little memory of how I got there. It's getting dark now. I unlock the vehicle and climb inside, clamping my hands on the steering wheel, eyes staring vacantly ahead.

I thought maybe Hazel had just said she was seeing someone else in order to make me jealous, or to keep me at bay. Alas, no. The bastard's real.

What's the state of their relationship? Has he been to the house yet? Has he met Mia? Has Mia been told to call him *Daddy?*

Bile rises to the back of my throat.

I reverse out of the parking space and pull away, a hollow feeling in the pit of my stomach. Once out of the hospital grounds, I turn right and immediately hit traffic lights.

I sit there, brooding.

A sudden jolt of rage surges through me and I scream, pummeling the steering wheel with my fists. I bury my head in my arms and groan.

When I look up, the light has changed to green. A horn blasts behind me. I pull myself together and move on.

* * *

I navigate the series of roundabouts that takes me out of the city and back onto the motorway. Once in the flow of traffic I relax a little. Turn on the radio. The dance music's relentless beat makes my growing headache worse, so I switch it off again.

Glancing at the dashboard clock, I groan. It's almost Mia's bedtime already, and I wanted to spend a little time with her first. God, I miss her so much. I'm not sure if Hazel has told her any awful things about me, but I still see the love in Mia's eyes every time I come and pick her up. She doesn't judge me, she doesn't think less of me. She's the only thing in this world keeping me sane right now.

The bright lights of oncoming traffic make me realize just how tired I am and I yawn, rubbing my eyes.

A tiny white dot. On the back of my eyelids, in the center of my vision.

My eyes snap open, heart pounding painfully in my chest.

A white dot.

Not stars this time, not little colored circles. This thing is different. It has substance.

No, it's just an afterimage from the headlights of oncoming vehicles, surely? That whole experience with Zack has made me paranoid.

I close my eyes to check. There it is again—a pinprick of light in the black.

A loud horn blast causes my eyes to spring open and I realize, glancing at the instrument panel, that my speed has dropped below fifty. Glaring headlights fill the rearview mirror. I pull over to the inside lane to let the vehicle pass.

You'll see.

I shudder.

Maybe my niggling headache has developed into a full-blown migraine. It makes sense, given that I've barely slept in the last two days. But Zack's pop-eyed prophecy continues to haunt me.

You'll see.

I blink hard, but it's all too brief for me to see anything. I glance in the rearview mirror to check that there are no vehicles behind me. Holding the steering wheel as steady as I can, I take a deep breath and close my eyes.

It comes into focus after a moment. A ball of light. Only this time it's different. It's more than doubled in size, and it's expanding and deflating ever so slightly, with the steady rhythm of a living, breathing creature.

Then, with a sudden pulse, its mass increases once more.

As fear compresses my chest, I'm unable to shake the feeling that this thing is coming for me.

CHAPTER 6

When I open my eyes I discover that the car has dipped into the next lane. It's bearing down on the vehicle in front.

"Shit, shit, shit!"

Swerving frantically to avoid a collision, I whip back into my own lane. I take a moment to get my bearings, and then continue along the motorway at a steady pace.

There's no ball of light at all, of course. It's merely psychological. Zack's scaremongering has made me imagine it, and nothing more. Like when someone gets you so spooked you start seeing figures in the dark where there are none.

I close my eyes quickly, just to check.

Okay, so it's definitely there. No doubt about it. And the surface area of what now looks like a white blob is steadily expanding.

Jesus Christ. What the hell is this thing?

Everything I think I know suddenly readjusts itself as I realize that Zack is not a madman, after all.

And I will absolutely have to stop blinking.

Even as I think it, I blink.

Damn it! I have to override the instinct somehow. I widen my eyes and keep them there, but after thirty seconds it's already getting uncomfortable. I relax them a little and my eyelids flutter, demanding to blink.

Agh! This is impossible. I'm never going to be able to do this. I relent, blinking quickly.

I think I can see the blob of light even then.

Really, though, what kind of damage can a little thing like this do? What's the harm in it? Granted, it looks pretty big to me right now, but that's because it's on the surface of my eye. Specks of dust or grit look quite large when you see them floating across your vision, but that doesn't mean they're going to kill you.

Yes, this thing is there, and it's getting bigger, but it's nothing to freak out about. It's just a microorganism or something. In reality it has to be, what? Half the size of a bed bug, maybe. If that.

No big deal.

I turn up the heating. Rummage through the pack of mints in the cup holder and pop one into my mouth. The headache is easing a little now.

A series of images flood my mind, of Zack and the knife and the blood and the eyelid sliced at the corner. All to the soundtrack of Zack's voice repeating *you'll see,* over and over and over…

Whatever. Even if Zack isn't crazy, he is at the very least weak-minded. So he saw a little blob in his vision and felt the need to cut off his eyelids? No, sorry. This isn't going to affect me like that. It seems sensible to refrain from blinking for now, certainly, but I'm not going to lose my mind over it. I've seen no evidence that this thing is in any way harmful.

A distant car horn blasts, causing me to jump and blink at the same time. I would have thought it an impossible task to keep my eyes from blinking for such a sustained period if I hadn't recently spent all that time with Zack. I have a new-found admiration for the guy.

I'm driving too slow for the road again. I've been concentrating so hard on not blinking that I've neglected to pay attention to my driving. Passing a sign that reads, 'FOR SERVICES, TAKE NEXT LEFT', I flip the turn signal and steer off the carriageway.

CHAPTER 7

The main food court area of the service station is swarming with travelers grabbing something to eat from the Burger King or the KFC or the Subway. I carve a path through the crowds, tempted by the smell of cooked food, and follow signs to the bathroom. Fruit machines and video games beep and whistle as I pass the amusement arcade.

Once inside the men's bathroom I approach the row of basins and lean close, examining myself in the dirty mirror. There isn't anything obviously wrong with me. The bathroom's sickly yellow downlighting doesn't help, accentuating the bags under my bloodshot eyes, but the general state of my appearance isn't anything out of the ordinary.

I study each eye in turn, then, realizing I don't even know which eye is infected, close my left eye and cover the right with the palm of my hand.

The white light twinkles like a solitary star in the night sky.

I switch hands and close my right eye. There it is again.

I gasp, staring in horror at my reflection. There are two of these things, one in each eye, but when I close both eyes they seem to blend together as one.

The man at the next basin along frowns at me. I turn and enter a vacant stall, locking the door. I need to take a moment to really study this thing. I inhale deeply, inadvertently breathing in the unpleasant odor inside the stall, and close my eyes.

It hasn't increased in size since the last time I saw it. But as I watch, the throbbing mass noticeably enlarges with each pulse. Screwing my eyes tightly shut seems to sharpen my focus on it. The glare from the halo of white light surrounding it has lessened, and I can see much clearer now what I'm looking at.

It's more than just a blob or a ball, that much is immediately obvious. For a start, it isn't circular. There are dozens, if not hundreds, of narrow, convulsing outgrowths protruding from both sides of the undulating mass, very much like…

My heart pounds in my chest, its rhythm matched by the pulsing at my temples. Yes, it's clear to me now. *Dear God.*

What I'm looking at are wriggling legs.

Now that I have a clearer picture of its form, I notice other details. The body is almost oval in shape, except that the base is slightly elongated, giving it the appearance of an imperfect lozenge. There are what appear to be pincers emerging from the front end. Two quivering, threadlike protuberances extend out from this dome-like extension to form its antennae.

I'm witnessing the metamorphosis of some kind of insect.

Opening my eyes, the afterimage of the blindingly white critter projects itself onto the door of the stall. I stare in disbelief until the image fades, replaced by the scrawled musings of a dozen bored former occupants.

A pang of fear twists my gut. I can't possibly pick up Mia now—I'll infect her, too. Damn it, Zack was right. I should have listened to him. I have to get back to King's Hill and receive the antidote. That is, of course, assuming I can keep my eyes open for that long…

I burst out of the stall and run for the exit. Stumbling out of the door, I merge with the throng of people headed for the food outlets, the stench of sour urine replaced by the inviting scent of cooked food. Arcade machines bleep, babies cry, newspapers rustle.

There are people everywhere.

Ahead of me, a toddler fights to get out of her father's arms. Her eyes lock onto mine, and she stops wriggling.

I force a smile, aware that my wide, unblinking eyes must look as terrifying as Zack's. To my surprise, the little girl laughs, holding out her arms.

As her chubby little fingers reach for me, I gasp in realization and jump back, almost slamming into a passer-by who manages to navigate around me at the last moment.

"Don't touch me!" I cry.

The little girl's face begins to crumble.

I spin around, surrounded by people going about their business. Haven't they heard? Do they all *want* to die?

"Don't touch me!" I yell, raising my arms. "Don't any of you people touch me, okay?"

I look around at the sea of puzzled faces, a wave of burning shame washing over me as I realize that now I'm the crazy person I thought Zack to be. A woman pushing a stroller freezes, glancing at me in terror. She slowly backs away. The father of the toddler shakes his head in bewilderment and wanders off. The crowd around me ripples away as people get the message.

Maybe they think I have a bomb strapped to my chest or something. And if this thing is as dangerous as Zack claims, then that might not be too far from the truth.

A security guard near one of the food outlets speaks into his radio and heads in my direction.

"Give me room," I demand, barreling through the crowd. "Get out of my way!"

I burst into a run, bolting through the food court in a direct line to the exit. The security guard quits following and watches me leave. As I pass through the automatic doors I expect to be confronted by another guard or two, but there are none around. I make it back to my car without incident and jump inside, slamming the door.

I fall back into the seat, releasing a sigh of immense relief. Then, thinking of something, I open the glove compartment and reach inside. Rifling through the junk, I find a matchbook and flip it open, pulling out two matches and snapping off the heads.

Craning my neck so that I can see my reflection in the rearview mirror, I lift my left eyelid and bring the matchstick in close. It tickles my eyelashes and I flinch. I'm not entirely sure I can do this—I've never even been able to wear contact lenses due to my refusal to bring my fingertip into close proximity with my eyeball—but I have to try.

Propping my eyelid open with the matchstick, I lodge the other end beneath my eye at the base of the socket. To my astonishment, it holds.

I grab the second match and bring it to my right eye, holding the eyelid in place. As I maneuver it into position, I accidentally poke myself in the eye.

"Ah! Shit! Jesus!"

My eye closes on instinct, granting me a quick flash of the creature. Its sheer size shocks me—I've forgotten quite how much it grew as I studied it in the bathroom.

Continuing on with a renewed sense of purpose, I wedge the matchstick into place. The broken end presses painfully into the soft flesh beneath my eye, and I find that I have to wince slightly to keep the matches in position. It's far from an ideal solution, but it'll have to do.

I reverse out of the parking space and pull away, my eyes half shut, the matches encroaching on my vision. As I look around for the exit, I realize just how little I can actually see. It's like trying to drive through the bars of a jail cell. I carefully navigate my way onto the road and turn right at the roundabout, across the bridge that will take me to the northbound carriageway and back to the hospital.

As I drive over a bump in the road, one of the matchsticks falls into my lap. The other stick loses its grip on the base of my eye socket and jitters before me, trapped in the folds of skin above my eye. I pull it out and throw it into the footwell. So much for that idea.

My eyes immediately sting from lack of moisture, and a sickening doubt surfaces. Even in good traffic it will take another half an hour to reach the hospital, and it's past rush hour now, but still...

My eyelids flutter uncontrollably as I try to keep them open, the stinging sensation intensifying. Car headlights and overhead streetlights streak together in a blur of abstract shapes, and I know that if I don't blink soon I'll crash the car anyway. I have no choice.

I close my eyes. Soothing relief is replaced by terror as the creature expands in one sudden, pulsing movement, almost doubling in size until it covers more than half my field of vision.

The level of detail is extraordinary. I can clearly see the pincers now, and the probing antennae. What looks like a hard shell covers the creature's body, which is divided into sections, each with its own set of wriggling appendages.

My eyes open, but within seconds the lids are heavy and desperate to close again. I drop my head in defeat, and then see something: Zack's box cutter on the passenger seat, the gunmetal of its casing helping to camouflage it against the gray of the seat fabric. It must have fallen from the pocket of Zack's pajama pants.

I imagine lifting the knife to my eye. Making an incision in my eyelid with the blade.

No. I shudder. That is not an option. And yet, I find myself reaching over and grabbing the knife anyway. Indicating right and turning onto the slip road, I slide the lever on the side of the knife up and down, extending and retracting the blade.

The stinging in my eyes is back with a vengeance. It comes in waves, I've noticed. Sucking the air through my teeth, I grip tight to the steering wheel, trying to ride out the pain. But it's considerably worse than before.

My eyelids spasm. I've never wanted to blink more in my life. Eyelashes flutter in my vision as my eyes try to close. It's going to require all of my concentration to keep them open, and I'm bearing down on the motorway, fast.

I feel a yawn coming on and stifle it. *Wait*—I can yawn without closing my eyes, right? I feel stupid not instantly knowing the answer. I widen my mouth to force the yawn and it comes, bathing my eyes in moisture. It's heaven, and the stinging eases off. Tears glisten across my sight, smearing all light sources into streaks as I approach the carriageway.

I push down on the accelerator, moisture welling in my eyes at the bottom of my sight, and, placing the knife on the passenger seat, join the flow of traffic headed north.

CHAPTER 8

Turning off the main road and into the grounds of King's Hill hospital, an incredible weight lifts from me. God knows how, but I made it. I'm here.

As I pull up outside the main terminal building and survey the scene, my heart lurches into my throat. There are no lights on in the lobby. No patients or staff milling around outside. The automatic revolving door is no longer turning.

The hospital appears to be closed.

I leap out of the car. My eyes, upon hitting the cool night air, feel like lumps of glass in my sockets. I run to the entrance, pushing on one of the glass panel doors, but it's locked in place.

"No, no, no!"

My frantic gaze lands on the side entrance to the left of the revolving doors. A burly security guard is locking the door from inside the building.

I'm there in an instant, charging the door, slamming into the glass with my full force. The door moves a few inches before meeting resistance. The guard is shoving back on the other side, staring at me through the glass.

"You can't come in," he shouts. "Hospital's on lockdown."

"It's an emergency. I need to see someone."

The guard fumbles with his keys, trying to keep the door shut while turning the lock. "No, I'm sorry. You'll have to go elsewhere. It's a viral outbreak."

I push the door open a little and slide my foot through the gap. The guard matches my force on the other side. Hitting a stalemate, we lock eyes through the glass. With mounting alarm, I realize that the guard isn't glaring at me; his wide eyes are a sign of his infection.

A cold terror shoots through me. How widespread has this thing become? And what about Hazel? Has it reached her yet?

"I've got it, too," I yell. "It's too late for me. Lock me inside with everyone else."

The guard shakes his head.

Crying out in frustration, I slam my fist against the glass. "Come on, man!"

When I look back, the guard's eyes flash with terror.

I stare at him, confused. The man's face is instantly panic-stricken. He seems to be hitching in air. He grabs his nose, squeezing his nostrils together, and suddenly I realize what's happening.

The guard is trying to hold back a sneeze.

"Oh, God," he mutters, a note of almost heartbreaking despair in his voice. He pauses for a moment, and then sneezes.

His eyeballs explode in a fountain of blood and viscera that splatters the pane of glass between us.

I reel in horror, my mouth agape.

My view of the guard now obscured, I push the door open and step tentatively inside. I find him on the floor, writhing in agony, hands covering his face. Vitreous fluid erupts from between his splayed fingers. Gargled screams emanate from his throat.

"Help!" I call out. "Someone, please! Quick!"

I kneel over him, my mind numb with helplessness. The guard reaches out, grabbing my hand. I look at his face and recoil. His eye sockets are a mess of pulped jelly.

Grimacing, I turn away. The beige vinyl floor is streaked with blood. Four, maybe five other bodies are strewn across the lobby.

The guard falls silent. His grip loosens.

I let go of his hand, an overwhelming feeling of despair washing over me. Am I next? Is Hazel?

Pounding footsteps. I look up. A second security guard slows to a stop as he discovers his fallen colleague.

"Lock down the hospital," I say, scrambling to my feet. My legs are unsteady. "This thing mustn't get out."

I head for the light of the main corridor beyond the lobby. Pushing through the double doors, I'm immediately confronted by an old woman in a hospital gown. She stumbles toward me, eyes bulging, arms outstretched like a zombie from one of my video games. I step around her, slipping in a puddle of blood and losing my footing for a moment.

Two men in white coats rush past me.

"Doctor Roman?" I ask. They ignore me, continuing on their way. The corridor elbows to the right and I follow it, checking signs on the walls. I pass the cafeteria, which is shut up for the night.

A man argues with a female doctor some distance down the corridor. "That's the best you can do?" he cries. "My little girl's dying in there."

The doctor touches his arm and says something that causes the man to raise his arms in dismay.

I come to a stairwell and scan the floor plan fixed to the wall. The Clinical Research Ward is on the fourth floor. I charge up the steps two at a time.

Blood curdling screams echo down the stairwell from another level.

Pulling out my phone, I call Hazel. It starts ringing. "Come on, come on!" After a short while the answering service kicks in. I leave a message asking her to get back to me.

On the landing between floors I come across a woman in a nightdress, slumped against the wall with her head on her chest. "You okay?" I ask.

She doesn't move. I lift her head and recoil. Her eyes are missing.

I continue up the stairs to the fourth floor, following signs to the ward. The corridor is dark and eerily silent. The door to the ward is ajar. I step through, a sour taste in my mouth.

The sight that greets me steals my breath away. Streaks of blood smear the walls and floor in elaborate splash patterns, as if the corridor is part of an installation in a modern art gallery. A gurney has tipped over. The area around the reception desk is littered with spilled paperwork and box files.

My feet feel like they are encased in cement. "Doctor Roman?"

Shuffling forward, I pass the entrance to a bay, sealed off with a heavy glass door marked ISOLATION. I peer inside.

Rows of beds, their occupants unmoving. Bedsheets spattered with blood.

RESTRICTED AREA, a sign beside the door reads. I try the handle and the door slides open. I hesitate on the threshold, and then enter. A chill runs through my bones as I confirm what I'd already suspected—there's a corpse in every bed.

Every patient has holes where their eyes should be. I approach the nearest body, that of a man wearing blue-and-white striped pajamas. The vague suggestion of eyeballs fills the sockets, the blood around this mess of jelly still fresh.

My gaze stops on the man's eyebrow piercing, and my veins fill with ice. It's Zack lying there.

My head spins. I'm suddenly overcome with sorrow.

"I'm so sorry, buddy..."

A feeling of rage builds within me. Where's Doctor Roman? Why hasn't he administered the cure to any of these patients?

Glancing across to the next bed, it's immediately clear that the body of the female patient lying there is in a more advanced state of decay—her eye sockets are hollowed out. Horrified but intensely curious, I move around the bed, leaning over to get a better look at what remains of her face.

The optic nerves have been shredded, the eye muscles torn away. Whatever could have done such unspeakable damage?

I gasp—there's movement. Inside the skull, on the mass of tissue that I assume to be the base of the woman's brain.

What I see is an insectoid abomination—a hybrid of slug and cockroach. A tube of flesh with a hard black shell and wriggling legs. It's about an inch and a half long from the tip of the antennae to the base of its swollen abdomen. Its head twitches, pincers moving rapidly. A set of strong jaws extend from its mouth and I realize, drawing back in terror, that the creature is *eating*.

I stare in goggle-eyed disbelief, the hideousness of my discovery shocking me into a state of paralysis. These creatures have no interest in a person's eyes.

They want what's behind them.

CHAPTER 9

Turning right at the end of the ward corridor, I come across a stainless steel sliding door with a built-in glass panel. I look inside.

A laboratory. Storage cabinets stand open with various chemicals stacked in neat jars on the shelves. A wiry little man in a lab coat rushes back and forth, examining slides through a microscope and switching them. The lab is a mess of flasks and various other medical instruments scattered across the work surfaces.

I slide the door open and step inside. "Doctor Roman?"

Oblivious to my presence, the man disposes of a slide and whirls between benches, frantically filling test tubes from a flask of liquid.

I ask again. "Are you Doctor Roman?"

The man glances up. His eyes appear almost comically wide behind a pair of safety goggles. He grunts and continues about his work, sweating profusely.

"I'm infected," I say.

He whips off his safety goggles and looks at me. "I didn't think," he says, "that you were staring so hard because you had a crush on me."

I wince as I notice that Roman's eyes are held open with pins that penetrate his eyelids, fixing them in place. "I was told that you can help me. That you have the antidote."

The doctor tends to something on the table before him, his actions fueled by a nervous energy that gives him a jittery appearance.

"Doctor? The antidote?"

Roman meets my eye. He places a hand on his chin and studies me, bony fingers dancing across the side of his face. "I think," he says, "you need to sit down."

I remain standing. "Please, I can't keep this up much longer. Are you going to help me or not?"

"You have to understand something, Mister…"

"Matheson. Ajay."

"I've been working tirelessly, Mr Matheson. Tried everything, tested everything. These little buggers… they're untouchable."

I'm stunned into silence for a few heartbeats. "Wait—what?"

Struck by a sudden sensation of vertigo, I grab a nearby stool and fall onto it. It doesn't seem to help. My head spins, trying to right itself in an upside down world. "You have a cure, though, right? I mean, that's why you recalled all the trial subjects…"

He snorts. "Oh, I haven't given up, as you can see. I have one last idea. In fact, you're just in time to watch me test it." He holds up a test tube and examines the liquid inside. "There's a very good chance that even if the critters don't kill me, this stuff will. But hey, ho."

I watch with mounting alarm as Roman grabs a syringe, unscrews the hub and affixes an incredibly fine needle.

"And if it doesn't work?" I ask. "What then?"

Roman reaches for a small box, hurling it across the worktop to me.

I remove the lid and look inside. It's full of pins, the same type that are keeping Roman's eyes open.

"Oh, God," I say. "No. No, I just can't."

Roman frowns. "You know, it's perfectly possible to sleep with your eyes pinned open. The brain ignores sight stimulus when asleep. You'll just get very dry eyes and the occasional corneal abrasion."

I replace the lid. "That's not a long-term plan, though, is it? I can't keep my eyes open forever."

"That's why I'm hoping this will work." He fills the syringe with liquid from the test tube.

I'm not sure I want to be here for this. Just the sight of the needle is making me feel weak. "What is this creature, Doctor? Where did it come from?"

Roman studies the liquid in the syringe and taps the barrel. "I was working on a synthetic wonder drug. With the potential to cure many human ailments, not just dry eye disease. Unfortunately the organic component—I extracted it from the intestines of pigs—contained a parasite that was replicated during the genetic modification."

"Meaning what?"

"Meaning, I unknowingly created a monster. When the trial subjects mentioned a dot in their vision, I figured it was just an afterimage. Or floaters caused by the steroid entering the eye. It's quite common to complain of things in your vision in the hours following an injection, you see. But that's when I started seeing the blasted thing myself. And of course, I hadn't been administered the drug."

He drops into a chair and leans back, holding the needle up to his eye.

"Oh Christ," I say, looking away.

"It's okay, I'm not injecting it directly into the eyeball itself."

I glance back, relieved.

"No, just the meaty part in the corner."

My stomach rolls. I grimace, turning away. From the corner of my vision I see the doctor pushing down on the plunger. I've never wanted to close my eyes more in my life.

Roman cries out in agony, and then all is quiet. I can't bear it. My legs jiggle and bounce. I rock back and forth, fingers laced together.

"All done," Roman declares cheerfully. "That wasn't so bad."

I groan as I exhale. My hands are trembling. I look back in time to see the doctor pulling the pins out of his eyelids. "Oh, shit…" I shield my vision. "Now what?"

Roman places the pins on a lab cart and flexes the muscles around his now untethered eyes, preparing himself. "Now we test it."

He flares his nostrils, clears his throat, and then, remaining perfectly still, closes his eyes.

I hold my breath.

A moment later, Roman's eyes snap open. His face gives nothing away.

"Well?"

"Biologically," Roman says, "the creature is remarkably well-equipped." He turns and marches toward a desk at the back of the lab. "It thrives in all toxic environments."

"Did it not work? What happened?"

Roman picks up the receiver of an old-fashioned rotary dial telephone. "It's moving at an accelerated pace!" He punches in a number and waits. "It's Doctor Roman," he says into the receiver. "Red Alligator has bolted." He listens for a moment, his face flickering with emotion. "I understand."

He replaces the receiver.

"What was that?" I ask.

Roman steps around from behind the desk. All the nervous energy seems to have drained from him. "I'm sorry, Mr Matheson. I'm so terribly sorry."

"What's Red Alligator?"

His gaze drops to the floor, his face crumbling. "They're coming."

"What? Who?"

"You have to understand, I did everything I could."

"Who's coming?"

"This has to be contained. I have a duty, as the instigator of the virus. This is so much bigger than you or me or anyone at this hospital. A parasite like this, that's transmitted by touch—it could be the end of us all."

"Who's coming?"

"It's why I ordered all the original test subjects back to the hospital. I knew that pretending I had a cure would lure them back."

"Doctor. Who was on the end of that line?"

"I'm so sorry," he says, fumbling for the pins on the lab cart. "There's nothing anyone can do now." He lifts one of the pins to his left eye, but his hand is trembling.

"Wait, maybe I can help—"

Roman misses his eyelid and stabs the pin directly into his eyeball. Screwing up his eyes, he howls in pain.

"Don't!" I scream. "No! Be careful!"

The doctor clasps his hands to his face, a torrent of blood exploding between his fingers. He tumbles back onto the lab cart, sending flasks and test tubes crashing to the floor. I lurch after him but he topples sideways, hitting the floor tiles and writhing among the pieces of shattered glass.

"Doctor?"

I drop to the floor beside him. Roman stiffens, and then stops moving entirely, hands falling away from his face. His eyes have been obliterated, almost as if someone has chewed them up and spat the pieces back into his empty sockets.

I turn away and vomit.

CHAPTER 10

The corridor of blood looms ahead as I stagger through the ward, feet numb, sight impaired by a pea-souper that has descended like a thick curtain across my vision. Falling, defeated, against the reception desk, a whimper of despair escapes my lips.

I relax my eyelids, letting them hang over my sight, millimeters from closing. My eyelashes flicker before me in uneasy suspension. The pain abates for a moment.

As my eyes open fully, the fog has cleared a little but the stinging sensation has returned, more intense this time. My eyes click as they move in their sockets. I spy a water cooler in the darkness of the hallway and edge toward it, shuffling past the isolation bay and resisting the urge to look inside.

Filling a plastic cup, I gulp down its contents and fill it again, dropping back against the wall, the cool water soothing my throat. Blots of light spring up in the periphery of my vision as the stinging reaches the apex of its torture and, just as it feels like I have no choice but to blink, I widen my eyes even more.

The water works its magic, supplying my eyes with a coating of moisture, and if my pain is a mountain then I've crested the summit and am already on the descent. I slide down the wall until I'm sitting on the cold vinyl, knees drawn up, head buried between my hands. The throbbing at my temples vibrates through my fingertips. Relaxing my eyelids again, I feel my mind clearing, calmed by the steadying rhythm of my breathing.

The creature flashes before me.

I jerk awake, heart bashing against my ribcage. *Good God*, is it that easy to doze off?

The white afterimage imprinted on my sight tells me that I don't have long—the bug now fills the entire breadth of my vision. How many blinks does that afford me before my eyeballs explode like Zack's or Doctor Roman's? A dozen, maybe? If that?

Pulling out my phone, I try Hazel again. No answer. I scroll through the list of recent calls and tap another number.

My breath catches in my throat as the line connects.

The dragon's voice. "Hello?"

"Brenda, it's Ajay. Can I speak to her?"

Silence on the other end. I can almost sense the bitterness, the hostility.

"She's been crying," Brenda says at last. "Wondering where you are."

"I know. Please, just put her on."

I wait, hearing a muffled conversation in the background. Mia's voice. Tears prick my eyes, and instinctively I want to blink them away. Instead I roll my eyes around, giving them a moisture bath.

"Daddy?"

The tears tumble to my cheeks. "Peanut, it's me."

"Where are you, Daddy? I want you to read my bedtime story."

"I know, baby, and I'm sorry, but I won't be able to make it there tonight."

"Aww," she moans, beginning to cry.

"Hey, hey, it's okay…"

"You promised."

"I know. You'll have a sleepover at Granny's, though. That's good, isn't it?"

She sighs. "Yeah."

"Listen, make sure you get your pajamas on like a good girl when Granny asks, all right?"

"I've already got them on."

"Ah, good. Are they the Supergirl ones?"

"Yes, but I forgot the cape."

"Oh, that doesn't matter. It just means you won't be able to fly around catching bad guys tonight."

Mia giggles. "Don't be silly, Daddy."

"I'm sorry. Now make sure you clean your teeth before bed, okay?"

"Okay. I love you too, Daddy."

I laugh. She's said it like that for as long as I can remember, and I've always found it adorable. The laughter dies in my throat as I realize that this is the last time I'll hear her say it. "I love you too as well."

"Will I see you in the morning?"

Sucking in breath ready to speak, I discover there are no words. What can I say in response to that? "Yes. Yes, Mia, you'll see me in the morning."

"Yay! Okay, goodnight, Daddy."

My heart wrenches. *This is it.* I'll never know what she looks like all grown up. Or if she'll have a career looking after animals in some way, as I suspect she will. I'll never get to walk her down the aisle, or to give an embarrassing father of the bride speech, or to hold back the tears during the father-daughter dance. I've had the song, *I Loved Her First*, picked out since the day she was born.

"Goodnight, Peanut."

I hold on the phone until I hear a click, and the line goes dead.

CHAPTER 11

They're coming.

Doctor Roman's words echo through my mind, rousing me from my stupor. I have to reach Hazel and somehow get us out of here. I leap to my feet and exit the ward, the relative brightness of the corridor causing my eyes to ache as the light hits my retinas. Shielding my eyes with my hand, I call Hazel again. No answer.

Pushing on, I pass the elevator and press the call button, but the digital display above the door reads *88*. Given that there are no more than twelve floors in the hospital, I take this as a sign that the elevators are not in operation and burst through the double doors to the stairwell.

I vault down the stairs three at a time. On the first landing I step over the body of a groaning man, ignoring the natural impulse to stop and help. The guilt tortures me as I continue downward, but there's nothing I can do for the guy.

Reaching the ground floor, I explode out of the stairwell and into the main corridor. The scene before me is like something out of an asylum-based horror movie: wide-eyed staff guiding screaming patients down the hallway; fallen bodies littering the linoleum, bloody wounds where their eyes had been.

I lose my footing on the slippery floor and sail backward. The pain ricocheting up my spine as I land on my coccyx is immediately consumed by the terror of witnessing the creature lurching forward in my vision. I must have closed my eyes instinctively as I fell.

A cold sensation runs up my spine as something wet seeps through my clothes and across my back and arms. Pulling myself up onto my elbows, I see a rivulet of blood running centrally along the length of the corridor, like something from the killing floor of a slaughterhouse.

Grimacing, I roll out of the trough of blood and climb to my feet. The sweater clings to my back, causing me to shudder involuntarily. I press on. A loud shriek emanates from a nearby room, making me jump, but I make sure I don't blink. Moments later, a man turns the corner fast and almost collides with me. I flinch, but manage to keep my eyes wide the whole time. I'm finally getting the hang of this. Still, I know I won't be able to keep it up forever. It's only a matter of time before it's my blood flowing in rivulets down the corridor.

I reach the hallway leading to the oncology department, glad at last to be in a quieter part of the hospital. My relief turns sharply to fear as I see that the door to the ward has been wedged open with a plastic chair. The ward's access-controlled door had been my last hope—I imagined Hazel barricading herself and her patients inside, safe from infection.

I step over the chair and into oncology, almost too afraid to investigate.

"Hazel?"

The reception area is deserted, so too the office beyond. Calling for her again, I approach the entrance to a bay, heart in mouth, and peer inside. It's a similar story to the research ward: rows of patients looking, for all the world, like they're asleep in their beds, except for the small detail that their eyes are missing.

I check the adjoining bay, then the next, glancing at each body to make sure Hazel isn't one of them. I'm about to turn and leave the ward when I spy something out of the window, and freeze.

I move closer to the glass, unable to comprehend the horror of what I'm looking at. Now I know what Doctor Roman meant when he said *they're coming*.

The road approaching the hospital is entirely blocked by a convoy of armored trucks.

CHAPTER 12

I bolt out of the oncology department, sending the plastic chair crashing down the hallway. My heartbeat slams its rhythm in my ears. Entering the main corridor, I keep to one side to avoid the river of blood, passing an orderly pushing a screaming woman on a gurney. How the hospital staff manage to continue doing their jobs in the midst of what must surely seem like the apocalypse I don't honestly know.

Bursting through to the lobby, I skid to a halt. The area is crammed with people trying to escape. A group of agitated patients attempting to swarm the doors are being kept at bay by two security guards. Other people are crying, their arms raised in despair.

I have to find another exit. Turning back, I charge into the corridor. As the double doors swing shut behind me, an incredible explosion of noise causes me to stumble in shock. I spin around.

Breath trapped in my throat, I watch through the door's circular viewing window as patients tumble over each other to get away from the lobby entrance. Four—no, five men in green hazmat suits step through the exploded glass of the front door.

That constant and terrible noise, I suddenly realize, is the blast of automatic machine gun fire.

More men in hazmat suits pour into the lobby, firing indiscriminately. Howls of terror combine to form a single hellish scream. People are torn to shreds where they stand. The security guards are executed at point-blank range. Bodies drop to the floor in a haze of blood.

Patients scatter. A surge of people rush the exits at the rear of the lobby. Breaking from my horrified stupor, I turn and run just as the doors burst open, sending a tidal wave of people into the corridor.

The unrelenting peal of gunfire is deafening now.

I career mindlessly down the hall, convinced that I'll be brought down by a shower of bullets at any moment. Exploding through another set of doors, I send an elderly woman flying.

"Sorry," I call after her, a nonsense apology given that she'll be dead in a few seconds anyway.

The corridor elbows to the left and I follow it around. A long hallway stretches before me. Knowing that I'm vulnerable to attack on the straights, I duck into the first adjoining corridor and keep moving.

No longer feeling that I'm in the direct line of fire, I reach into my pocket and, with numb hands, feel for my phone. I have to warn Hazel.

For God's sake, she's dead already. Don't you get it?

"Stop it," I mutter aloud.

She doesn't answer the call.

There's an Emergency Exit sign above the door ahead of me. Pushing through, I turn into a narrow hallway of exposed brick that is surely on the perimeter of the building.

Distant screams emanate from the far end. Suddenly a man in a white coat appears, carrying two small children in his arms. He's running for his life.

I spin around and charge back the way I came.

A blast of gunfire. I reach the door and glance back. The doctor and two children are a bloodied mess on the floor.

A green-suited gunman emerges from the darkness, his weapon trained on me.

He opens fire as I throw the door wide and leap through. Breaking into a run, I look down to see if I've been hit.

Astonishingly, no. *I'm still alive!*

Then again, maybe not.

A movie scene pops into my head: Patrick Swayze in *Ghost*, chasing after the guy who just stabbed him, unaware that he's already dead.

A staircase. I hurtle up, up, *up.* Eyes wide. Feet pumping. Mind a flurry of panic. My body screams in pain. I can't catch my breath. *No stopping.* Up. Up.

Jesus Christ, those kids…

If I reach the roof then maybe I can get to street level via the fire escape. Even if they have the building surrounded, there's still a chance I can sneak away. I'll have to take it. In the outside world there'll be specialists, experts, falling over themselves to find a cure for my condition.

A final, steep staircase. I climb it to a barred door with *PUSH TO OPEN—ALARM WILL SOUND* stamped across it. I hesitate for a moment, and then depress the bar.

Stepping onto the roof, the squeal of the alarm is drowned out by a pulsing, choppy sound.

I scan the night sky for a helicopter but see nothing. Moving farther away from the door, the vast surface of the roof opens up to me. I stop dead.

An enormous, twin-engine cargo chopper has already landed on the roof, fifty feet or so from my current position. Hazmat-suited soldiers pour from the loading ramp at its rear.

Stumbling backward in horror, I turn and retrace my steps. The roof door has no handle on the outside. *Dear God,* it's locked. There's no way down.

No—it's on the latch. I pry it open with my fingertips and throw myself inside. Vault down the steps.

It's hopeless. There's no escape.

That voice is right, of course. They're everywhere. It's only a matter of time before they catch up with me. But thoughts of Mia spur me on. I have to somehow beat this thing and get back to her, especially if her mother…

No. I can't even think it.

The muffled rattle of gunfire soundtracks my frantic descent. Terrible images plague my mind—of men, women and children being flattened by bullets. I wish I could blink these thoughts away.

Emerging on a random floor, I scour the corridor for somewhere, *anywhere,* to hide. I freeze—a soldier stands at the end of the corridor, his back turned to me. I sneak around the corner only to find myself in the path of another green-suited gunman farther down the hall. I stand still—maybe the soldier hasn't seen me. It's impossible to tell with the man's face hidden behind both a gas mask and a plastic hood.

The soldier raises his weapon.

I pull open the nearest door and dive inside. A doctor's office. I'll have to work fast. Grabbing a wooden chair, I wedge the back rest beneath the door handle. Drag a heavy file cabinet across, blocking the doorway. Run to the window and look down.

My heart sinks. I'm still several floors up, and it's a sheer drop to the street below. An almighty thump rattles the door on its hinges.

Now what do I do?

Now nothing, I suddenly realize. This isn't about self-preservation anymore. If I've learned anything at all over the past few years, it's that it's about time I grew up and started putting my family first.

Today is not about getting back to Mia—it's about making sure that she survives.

I turn to face the door just as the chair jerks around beneath the handle. A short blast of gunfire shreds the lock.

This is it. Time to do my bit for humanity.

I take a deep breath.

A large hole explodes in the door.

Wait. This isn't right. If I'm going to die today, it has to be on my terms. I have to be the one to pull the trigger.

Okay. Let's do this.

Three…

Another burst of gunfire in the hallway.

Two…

The file cabinet topples forward as the door wedges open.

One...

I close my eyes.

CHAPTER 13

It's like looking at a bug through a microscope. The ridges across its back, the hair-thin claws at the end of its legs, the bulges of what may be wing pads at the base of the head.

I await death with resigned acceptance. *I love you, Mia.*

A cacophony of sounds: the crack of wood as the chair splinters. The door bashing repeatedly against the fallen filing cabinet. Far off screams. My own quickening breaths. Then suddenly, above all of this, something else. A very familiar little ditty.

The theme from *The Twilight Zone.*

Hazel!

My eyes snap open just as the door swings wide. I dive for cover behind it. A soldier in a hazmat suit waddles inside. Pinned against the wall, I watch as the soldier looks around, the plastic visor in his suit blocking the full range of his peripheral vision.

The phone continues ringing in my pocket. I can't just stand there and wait for the guy to turn around, so, charging from my hiding place, I leap on his back.

"Son of a bitch!" comes the muffled cry from inside the suit. I wrap my arms around him, trying to get him in a headlock, but I can't find his neck in the folds of plastic that make up the suit. The soldier thrashes around, trying to shake me off, but I hold on tight.

I want to reach down for his weapon, but that means loosening my grip. At that moment the soldier thrusts the stock of the machine gun upward in a stabbing motion, connecting under my chin.

My skull vibrates with the impact, teeth smashing together. The creature flashes before me as my eyes close instinctively.

Much more of this and I'm going to die anyway. With nothing to lose, I jump off the guy's back and shove him with everything I've got. He collides with the desk. I don't wait around.

In the corridor, the coast is clear. I barrel down the length of it, aware that the soldier will be right behind me. Turning the corner, I sneak into a doorway and find myself in a preparation room. Continuing through the next door I come to an operating theater, and beyond that, a recovery room.

I duck inside a curtain surrounding one of the beds and blanch at the sight of the enucleated corpse lying there. Pulling out my phone, the screen informs me that I have one missed call. I wait until I'm sure I've shaken the gunman and, hands trembling uncontrollably, fumble for the redial.

The phone rings. The breath wheezes from my lungs in short, panting gasps.

Incredibly, she answers. "Ajay?"

"Jesus. You're alive."

"Are you with Mia?" she asks.

"What? No. Where are you?"

She's breathless. Frantic. "Ajay, listen to me. I have something. Some kind of virus. I won't be coming home."

A wave of dizzying despair washes over me. It's crazy to feel that way—of *course* she's infected—but still, to have it confirmed…

"Are you there?" she says. "You need to keep her safe. She's your responsibility now."

"I'm *here*, Hazel."

"What?"

"I'm inside the hospital. I have it, too."

There's a long silence on the line, punctuated by distant gunshots. "No," she says.

"Yep. Afraid so."

"I told you to get back."

"Listen. Where are you?"

"I don't know. Near the concourse. They're all dead, Ajay. Everyone in the ward…"

"Stay hidden," I say. "I'm coming for you."

Ending the call, I creep out of the recovery room and pass through the operating theater to the doorway. The central corridor is empty. I dart out and, looking around, try to get my bearings.

A sign for the stairs. Quick and quiet, I enter the stairwell and descend the floors until I reach ground level. Emerging into the blood-soaked main corridor, I turn right toward the concourse, stepping over several bodies.

My veins fill with ice. Through the circular viewing window of the double doors ahead of me is the bulky outline of a hazmat suit. Headed this way.

I'm trapped.

There's only one option available to me. I drop to the floor and play dead.

The doors squeak open. I hold my breath, wide eyes buried in the fold of my arm.

The clump of heavy boots. My heart beats so hard I feel like I'm visibly vibrating. I'm suddenly glad that I slipped in the blood; all that claret over my back and arms *has* to look convincing, surely?

The footsteps stop beside me.

A boot kicks me hard in the ribs, causing air to expel from my throat in a gasp that I pray only I can hear. The soldier's full weight crushes the base of my back as he uses me as a stepping stone, and then he's gone, the clomp of his footfalls receding down the hallway.

I still daren't breathe.

Thirty seconds elapse. Has it been long enough? As I lift my head, the phone rings. The *Twilight Zone* theme tune.

She's wondering where I am. I have to answer it.

The double doors swing open.

No! I drop flat to the floor, playing dead again, but it's too late this time, I just know it.

"Oh, God!" A woman's voice. "Ajay? No…"

"Hazel?" I jerk my head around. She stands there, a vision in her blue-and-white uniform.

I climb to my feet. She's holding her phone. Her eyes are wide—partly, I suspect, with the shock of my sudden resurrection.

"My God, Hazel. I've found you!"

She looks me up and down. "Jesus. What happened to you?"

I glance at all the blood on my clothes and raise my hands in an *oh, this?* gesture. "It's okay, it's not mine."

She taps her mobile and my phone stops ringing.

I look at her and my eyes well up a little. I hope she can't tell. Her wide-eyed stare is a little disconcerting—I still expected her to be unaffected by all of this, somehow. "It's so good to see you."

The figure of a man appears in the doorway behind her, and I flinch. As the man moves into the light I see that he is tall and bespectacled, wearing pink scrubs. It's the doctor from oncology.

My heart plummets.

"It's okay," Hazel says on seeing my reaction. "This is Milton. He's with me."

Yes he is. Yes he is.

Milton nods an acknowledgement. I lift my fingers in a half-hearted wave.

"We'd better keep moving," Hazel says. She marches past me, Milton tagging close behind.

I turn and follow. "Where are you going?"

"Any grunts around here?" Hazel says.

"There were. Just…be careful."

She hugs the wall as we come to an adjoining hallway. Removing a compact from her pocket and flipping it open, she uses the mirror to check that the coast is clear. She nods to Milton and they keep going. It's like something out of a spy movie, and I'm impressed.

"So where are we off to?" I say, trying to keep up.

"Less of the chatter," Hazel whispers.

"Ophthalmology," Milton says under his breath.

I wasn't asking you, dickhead. "Opthal-what?"

"Ophthalmology," Hazel says quietly. "The eye ward. To see if we can find out what the hell this thing is."

"Oh, right. Makes sense." Stepping over more bodies slows me down. The others are through the next set of doors before I can catch up. I increase my pace and push through the doorway.

"It just so happens to be in the East Wing," Hazel says. "The remotest part of the hospital. It's the last place they'll come."

She checks that our path is clear again and signals for us to continue. We move steadily through the labyrinth of corridors, and I realize I'm completely lost. Thank goodness Hazel knows this building like the back of her hand.

"You think you can find a cure for this thing?" I ask in hushed tones.

"No," Hazel whispers back. It's not quite the answer I was hoping for. "But it's our only option, right? If we can convince these madmen we've found a cure, then there's at least a chance we can make it out of here alive."

I nod. Now is probably not the time to tell her that I think we should sacrifice ourselves for the sake of humanity if no cure can be found. Besides, maybe between us we really do have a shot at formulating an antidote. One of our number is a doctor, after all.

We arrive at the newly refurbished East Wing. The crackle of gunfire is distant now. This part of the hospital has a more high-tech design aesthetic, with open-plan areas consisting of warm woods and glass curtain walls. The occasional puddles of blood on the vinyl floor really ruin the luxurious feel.

"We're here," Hazel says, approaching a large door with the word *OPHTHALMOLOGY* frosted into the glass.

My attention is suddenly diverted by a man who appears on the other side of the door, his face a mask of panic.

He opens the door and steps out, hugging the wall in an attempt to keep as far away from us as possible. "Don't touch me!" he cries. "Don't any of you freaks touch me!"

"Hey," Hazel says. "It's all right. Calm down..."

"I'm clean, okay? I can blink. Look—" He blinks hard. "See? I'm not infected. So don't any of you people—"

The side of his head explodes in a shower of blood and brain fragments.

I jump at the sound of the machine gun blast. Milton screams. Hazel recoils as the man slumps to the floor.

A hazmat-suited gunman stands at the far end of the corridor.

He marches forward, weapon trained on us. More soldiers appear from the adjoining doorways, advancing on our position.

I'm frozen in terror.

"Please," Hazel says, stepping forward.

Jesus Christ, no.

My arm flies out to stop her. I have to do something, and fast.

CHAPTER 14

I step into the line of fire. "Red Alligator has bolted!"

Silence. Hazel and Milton stare at me in open-mouthed disbelief.

I survey the sea of soldiers, their weapons trained on me. My face falls.

After what seems like the longest moment, one of the soldiers breaks formation and orders the others to lower their weapons. He moves closer. "Doctor Roman?"

"Yes." I'm struggling to speak through trembling lips. "That's right. I'm the one who called you guys."

The soldier's voice is muffled behind his suit and gas mask. "You know how this works, Doctor. No survivors. If this parasite were to invade the general population…"

"Yes, yes, I'm well aware of that. What do you think I'm trying to prevent, here? I'm your best hope for a cure."

I look back at Hazel, who's glaring at me, and flash her a reassuring smile. I'd wink if I didn't think it might kill me.

The soldier pauses a moment, considering my words, then raises his weapon.

My hands fly up. "Wait!"

The soldier holds on me. "It's over, Doc. You gave the go-ahead."

"We're so close. I beg you. Just allow me and my team here a little time. We're onto something. That's why we've come here to…" Staring down the barrel of the gun, I forget the name of the department. Glancing back, I attempt to read it on the frosted glass. "Opha…Opthal…"

"Ophthalmology," Hazel says under her breath.

"Thank you, yes. Ophthalmology."

The soldier stares at me.

"I'm sorry," I say, "but the threat of imminent death makes me nervous."

The soldier huffs, fogging up the visor of his suit, then lowers his machine gun. "You have two hours, Doctor. If you've had no luck by then, we're coming in."

I'm so stunned to still be alive that it takes a moment for his words to register. "Thank you." I spring into action, pulling open the door and ushering Hazel and Milton into Ophthalmology. "Thank you very much." Backing into the department, I close the door and watch as the soldiers disperse.

When they're gone I fall back against the door, gasping with relief.

"That… was intense," Hazel says.

"I need a coffee," Milton says, visibly shaken. He moves over to a drinks machine.

Scrolling through the modes on my watch, I set the stopwatch for two hours. The digits start counting down.

We're in a waiting area with rows of empty chairs and a table piled high with magazines about motoring and fashion. A poster pinned to the noticeboard encourages patients to *LOOK AFTER YOUR EYES*.

Hazel holds her head in her hands, eyes glazed over. She snaps back to reality and looks at me. "What now?"

"I don't know. Any ideas?"

"Well, my original thought was that we should hook one of us up, start a course of intravenous antibiotics and monitor the progress. But given that we have only two hours, I guess that option's out."

"If it were that simple, then Roman would have found the antidote already."

"But there must be some kind of anti-parasitic drugs, toxic enough to kill these things."

"Again, Roman would have tried it already. And he did say they thrive in a toxic environment."

Hazel shrugs. "So what's your big solution?"

"I don't know, do I?" Milton wanders over, stirring a cup of machine coffee. "Shouldn't we be asking the good doctor, here?" I say.

Milton regards me with a blank expression and checks with Hazel. "What's he talking about?"

My eyes narrow as I realize that Hazel is blushing. A ball of terror forms in my gut.

She holds my look for a moment, then turns and walks away.

"Hazel?"

"Dude," Milton says, motioning to his own clothes. "Pink scrubs."

"Yeah, so?"

"So… I'm a ward assistant."

My mouth hangs open. The world spins dizzyingly. Unable to close my eyes and settle myself, I lose my balance and drop into one of the waiting room chairs.

Half of me wants to laugh, the other half to bash my head against the wall until my brains fall out.

I gather myself and chase after Hazel. Seeing me approach, she disappears through a doorway. I follow her inside.

It's a typical optometrist's examination room, with an eye chart on the wall and a big black chair at the far end. Hazel studies the various instruments and pieces of equipment. She doesn't look up as I enter.

"A ward assistant?"

"Yeah?" she says. "What?"

"Well, I mean, come on. How are we supposed to find a cure now?"

She examines a microscope on a portable cart. "I never said we'd find a cure. I just thought Ophthalmology seemed like the sensible place to come, that maybe we'd find some kind of temporary solution. You're the one who turned this into Mission: Impossible."

"Well I had to say something…"

"Yes, I know."

"They were going to kill us…"

"I'm aware of that."

"And to be fair, this was back when I thought we actually stood a chance of finding a cure. You know, given I was under the illusion that one of our number was a doctor."

Hazel shakes her head. "I'm not completely useless, you know. I do have some medical training."

"Of course. I'm sorry."

"And besides, it's worth a shot, isn't it? I mean, what else are we going to do? Watch the clock until those bastards come back and execute us?"

"Hey, listen, I totally agree. We'll do everything we can."

She sits at the microscope and adjusts the eyepiece.

"Is there anything I can do?" I ask.

She motions to the stool opposite her. "Place your chin on the rest and push your forehead against the plate."

I do exactly as I'm told. A bright light shines in my eyes and I feel a sudden and desperate urge to blink. "Sorry. Just give me a moment." I roll my eyes until the feeling passes. "Okay."

Hazel adjusts the lens and leans forward. "Stare straight ahead."

I look directly at her through a halo of light, her face partly obscured by the microscope. I'm so close I can feel the warmth of her breath on my skin. The aroma of her perfume sparks warm memories of home.

I want to close my eyes and breathe her in.

"I'm so sorry," I say. "For, you know, the way things worked out between us…"

"Ajay," she snaps. "Don't." She adjusts the lens once more.

"Do you see anything?"

She shifts in her seat. "Normally, this is where I'd ask you to blink, but don't."

I study the side of her face that's visible. One perfectly manicured eyebrow. The scar left by a stud in her nose when she was a teenager. The curve of her slender neck.

She pulls away from the eyepiece and pushes the cart to one side.

"Well?"

She rubs the backs of her hands. "Nothing."

"What do you mean, nothing?"

"I can't see anything."

I feel lightheaded. "It's right there. In my face. It's huge."

"I know. Same here."

"So how can you not even see it?"

"You know what it's like. A dust particle floating in your vision looks pretty enormous, but that doesn't mean it actually is."

"Yes, but you'd still see it through a microscope."

Hazel shrugs. "I'm as surprised as you are, Ajay. But I'm telling you, it's not there."

"How is that even possible?"

"Sensory adaptation," a voice interjects.

It's Milton, standing in the doorway.

"What?" Hazel says.

Milton removes his spectacles and inspects the lenses, looking for all the world like a doctor. "It's something I read about once," he says. "We should see the shadows cast by the blood vessels inside our eye, but because the brain's used to them always being there, it blocks them out. That's sensory adaptation. It's kind of why we stop hearing a continually ticking clock."

"O-kay," Hazel says. "So… what's the relevance, here?"

"Think about it. Why are eyeballs exploding all over the bloody hospital? It's not because this thing is on the surface of our eye. It's because it's *inside* it."

My stomach heaves. "Inside our eyeball?" *Ugh.* This is not the kind of thing I need to hear right now.

"Wait," Hazel says. "That makes sense. Anything blocking the light between the lens and the retina would be casting its own shadow."

"Right," Milton says. "Except that the blood vessels are stationary, and our eyes have adapted so that we don't see them. But this creature is constantly expanding."

I'm still struggling to grasp this concept. "So that's what we see when we close our eyes? This shadow?"

"Yes," Hazel says. "And as the bugs grow inside our eyes, there comes a point when the pressure gets too much, and…"

"Boom." Milton mimes his eyeballs flying out of his skull.

Everyone is silent for a moment, taking this in.

"Then I guess," I say, "the million dollar question is, how do we fight this thing if it's growing inside our eyeballs?"

A barrage of gunfire erupts from a distant part of the hospital.

"I don't know," Hazel says. "But we need to find a way, and fast."

CHAPTER 15

"So come on, then," Hazel says as we move through to a lounge area accessorized with colorful bean bags and cushions. "Brainstorm, people. How do we defeat this thing?"

Milton is already searching through cupboards and drawers. "Well, how do you kill bacteria? How do you kill germs?"

"Bleach," I say, sinking into an oversized sofa. "Bug killer. All toxic."

Hazel snorts. "I volunteer Milton to be the first to have bleach injected into his eyes."

"Extremes of temperature," Milton offers. "Hot and cold."

"But this is some kind of mutated monster bug, right?" Hazel says. "Normal rules don't apply."

I check my stopwatch. Just over ninety minutes left. It's quite hypnotic, watching the last remnants of your life dwindling away. "That's right. Doctor Roman said it was a genetically modified parasite."

"But it's still a living creature," she says. "It's not as if it's supernatural or something. Surely it can be killed?"

Milton comes over, hands hidden behind his back. "Guys, I've got something for you. Close your eyes."

We glare at him.

"Just kidding." He gives us a pack each. Inside the clear plastic bag is an eye bath and a bottle of saline solution.

Milton and Hazel open their packs. I can't even entertain the idea, and drop mine down the side of the sofa.

"Okay," Hazel says, pouring the solution into the eye bath. "So what's needed is some out-of-the-box thinking. Something even Doctor Roman wouldn't have thought about."

"What if it really *is* supernatural?" I say.

Hazel groans. "Out-of-the-box, Ajay, not out of this world."

"Seriously. Now there's a line of thinking Roman wouldn't have gone down."

Hazel rolls her eyes and looks over at Milton. "This is typical Ajay," she says. "Always bringing everything back to sci-fi or *X-Files* or whatever crap he's been watching lately."

"Thanks," I say.

"What? It's true. You'll be saying this thing came from outer space next."

I hesitate. "Well, now that you say it…"

Derisive laughter bursts from Hazel's mouth.

"But think about it. We don't know the origin of this thing. It could have crashed to Earth on a meteor or something and that's why nobody knows how to deal with it."

"Great," she says. "Thanks for your input, Ajay. We're saved. Let's all go home."

Milton fills his eye bath with saline solution, and then rests the container on the base of his eye socket. In one swift movement he seals it around his eye and tips his head up. I look on in awe.

Hazel fills her eye bath and lifts it to her eye.

I wince. "Be careful."

"It's fine," she says, rotating her eyes in their sockets.

"Come on, Ajay," Milton says. "You too."

I shake my head.

"He's sensitive about eye stuff," Hazel says.

"Then you really should be drinking lots of water," Milton says, switching to his other eye. "Need to hydrate those peepers somehow."

I nod. "Thanks, Doctor."

Hazel shoots me a look. I can't help but smile.

"Okay," she says, holding her stare. "Shoot. How do you kill something supernatural?"

I shrug. "I don't know."

"Brilliant."

"It depends. With ghosts, you call in an exorcist. Werewolves and shapeshifters, it's a silver bullet to the heart. And with vampires you have to behead them. Or you can poison them by infecting them with dead man's blood."

"Maybe that's it," Milton says. "You infect the thing that infects you. Infect it right back again."

"How?" Hazel says. "With what?"

Milton goes to say something, and then stops himself. His cheeks redden.

"Reapers," I continue, feeling sorry for the guy. "Now they are tough sons of bitches. They can't be stopped, or killed. And they can only be seen by the person they're coming to take."

"Yeah," Hazel says, placing her eye bath down on the coffee table. "Just like these little bastards."

Her words send a shiver down my spine. What if this creature is the Angel of Death, its shiny armor a black cloak, its pincers twin scythes. Once you're infected, there's no way back. You're marked for death, and it's coming for you.

"Dying," Milton says. "Maybe that's the solution."

"Awesome," Hazel deadpans. "You're a real pair of geniuses, you two."

Milton continues undeterred. "This thing wants brains, right? So what if the brain was no longer there as a target? A living brain, I mean. What if we did a *Flatliners* and died for a few minutes?"

Hazel shakes her head. "There's still chemical energy running through the brain for a few minutes after death. And to leave it even that long would risk brain damage."

"Besides," I say, "from what I saw of these things on the research ward, they're perfectly happy munching on dead brains."

"Yeah, Milton," Hazel says. "Thanks for another ingenious solution."

He shrugs. "Hey, I'm just spitballing. You wanted ideas."

"Yes, something workable. An inspired thought. Instead I have you two dimwits harping on about *Flatliners* and grim reapers."

"Well, I'm so sorry," he says. "We can't all be medical professionals. So where are all your clever ideas?"

Hazel sighs. "Yeah, well, I'm kind of screwed. I do all of my best thinking with my eyes closed."

I explode with laughter. She glares at me, but I can't help it. Nothing has ever seemed funnier. Tears stream down my face.

"At least he's hydrating his eyes," Milton says.

This only makes me laugh even harder. Through the glaze of tears I glance at my watch. One hour and fifteen minutes until the end of the world. It's hilarious! Nothing makes sense. What is reality anymore, anyway? A world of blood-smeared walls and brain-eating bugs and government-sanctioned slaughter?

My stomach starts to hurt and I don't want to laugh anymore, but now I can't stop.

I'm aware that Hazel and Milton are still bickering. Clearly they've been together longer than I thought — they're way beyond the cosy romance of the honeymoon period. I'm suddenly absolutely convinced that Milton lives in my old house, sleeping in my old double bed. Probably even on my side of the bed, given that Hazel has always insisted on sleeping on the right.

The laughter dies in my throat.

Sharp pain stings my eyes. I suck the air in through my teeth. *Wow.* That really hurts. Another wave, but this time it's so much more than stinging.

Shit. What the hell is wrong? A sudden jolt of incredible pain causes me to gasp loudly.

"Ajay?" It's Hazel, leaning over me. "Are you all right?"

My eye screams, desperate to close. Something scratches at my cornea. "Have a look," I say, pointing to my left eye. "Quick."

My eyelids flutter uncontrollably. Terror grips my heart. I'm not ready to die.

Hazel's finger hovers into view. I flinch instinctively.

"Careful," she says. "Take it easy."

She holds my left eye open with her thumb and forefinger. The pain is immense. Have I cut my eyeball, somehow?

Hazel's shoulders slump. "It's an eyelash."

"What?"

"A loose eyelash, that's all. On the white of your eye."

That's all? This single eyelash is going to kill me, doesn't she understand that?

"Hold still," she says, and only then do I realize how much I'm thrashing about.

"The eye bath!" Milton says. "That'll wash it out!"

"I can't."

"I mean it," Hazel says. "Hold still. I can get this."

Her fingernail looms in my vision. *Oh, God.*

I try pretending that I'm elsewhere, that this isn't happening. Has she got it yet?

"Almost there," she says.

My eyeball sears with pain. *Go on, then.* The pad of her finger hovers. What is she waiting for?

She touches the surface of my eye with a quick dabbing motion, and I blink.

"Ahh!" The creature leaps forward, all legs and scuttling motion.

My eyes are open again. And still intact, astonishingly. "Did you get it?"

"I don't know," Hazel says. She pulls a pen light from the breast pocket of her uniform and clicks the base to turn it on.

"No, wait…"

"Let me do this," she says, bringing the pen close. She shines it directly into my left eye, which is still so sensitive that the bright light is unbearable.

It's no use. My eye closes.

Instantly, I notice something incredible. The bug's growth has halted. It's no longer advancing on me. *What the hell?*

The bright light has made the creature stop in its tracks.

CHAPTER 16

"Ajay!" Hazel yells. "Ajay, for God's sake, open your eye!"

I stare in unbridled wonder at the creature suspended before me, its legs still wriggling, abdomen pulsing, antennae groping. It's alive but stationary.

"Ajay! What are you doing?"

Something else is happening now. The creature is pulling into sharper focus, the empty space around it widening. I clamp a hand over my other eye so that I can see it better.

My God...

The light flicks off.

I open my eye. "No! Turn it back on!"

"What?"

"Just do it!"

Hazel clicks the base of the pen and the beam of light shines directly into my left eye once more. I close it, watching in breathless, open-mouthed shock as the creature retreats.

"It's shrinking!"

"My God!" Milton calls out.

Hazel gasps. "You're kidding…"

She holds the light to my eye until, after a few seconds, the bug has shrunk to the size of the dot it had been when I first noticed it on the motorway.

"Grab some lights!" I cry, bolting up into a sitting position. "Quickly!"

Milton is already rummaging through drawers. He finds a pack of pen lights and gives two to Hazel and one more to me.

Flicking on both of the lights, I shine them into my eyes before shutting them. The creature in my right eye retreats just as before, until it matches the dot in my left eye. Even a sustained blast doesn't make the dots disappear entirely, but I'm able to rest my eyes, and it's heaven. Like an ice cold glass of water on a sweltering day.

I blink my eyes a few times just because I can.

"Incredible," Hazel says, and I look up to see her holding the lights up to her closed eyes. Milton cackles as he does the same.

I yawn, the moisture bathing my eyes. It's only when I close them that I realize just how sore my eyelids are. My entire life, I've taken for granted being able to close my eyes whenever I wanted. Well, never again. Now I truly know the joy of a moment's shut eye.

I inhale deeply, and then exhale. Sleep captures me in an instant.

Legs. Antennae. Mandible. Teeth.

I wake with a start. *No…*

The two pen lights are still in my grip, but the beams of light have slipped.

When I close my eyes the creature hurtles forward, as large in my vision as it has ever been. Gasping, I bring the lights closer. The bug retreats again, until it's merely a dot of light in the darkness.

"Is this it?" Milton says. "Have we found a cure?"

"They're still there," Hazel says. "And I'm pretty sure Doctor Roman would have known about their aversion to light."

I decide to test my discovery. I turn off the pen lights and blink. The creature leaps forward, halfway to me in an instant. One more blink and I'm dead.

My eyes snap open. "Oh, no…"

"What?" Hazel and Milton are staring at me.

Hurriedly, I turn the pen lights back on and shine them into my eyes. Closing them, I watch as the creature retreats to a dot. "The light makes them angry, or… or gives them fuel. As if they're solar-powered or something."

"Oh, shit," Milton exclaims, already closing his eyes and testing it. He opens them sharply. "The light charges them up," he says. "So that they move faster next time."

The pen lights shake as my hands tremble. "Whereas before we had a short period of time before they progressed from a dot to right in our faces, now they're there in the blink of an eye."

Hazel drops her pen lights on the table as if they're contagious. "Maybe," she says, "we should only use the lights to keep them at bay. Until then, we keep our eyes open."

"Agreed," I say.

"Wait." It's Milton. "This has got to mean something. What if we're just using the wrong kind of light?"

"Explain," Hazel says.

"Well, radiation kills microorganisms, and that's what this thing starts out as, right? And on the oncology ward we use—"

Hazel finishes his thought. "Ultraviolet light therapy to kill cancer cells! Holy shit, Milton, you're a genius!"

She runs over and kisses him on the lips. I'm incredibly relieved, of course, that Milton has potentially come up with a solution that will save us all, and yet the feeling that hits me the hardest is one of intense jealousy.

"Okay," I say, "so where do we find a source of ultraviolet light?"

Hazel smiles. "I know just the place."

CHAPTER 17

"They use UV light to sanitize medical instruments before operations," Hazel says, marching into the operating theater. "So we should find some right around…" She scans the worktops, and then finds what she's looking for. "…here!"

She picks up a light wand and presses the button on the side. A tube of UV light illuminates. "So, I'll play doctor. Who wants to be the guinea pig?"

Milton steps up.

"No," I say. "Test it on me first. You know… in case it doesn't work."

Hazel and Milton stare at me with quizzical looks on their faces.

"You guys have to get back to Mia," I say. "You're her parents, now."

Hazel's face softens.

Milton nods. "Thanks, dude."

Climbing onto the operating table, I shift my weight, trying to get comfortable. I exhale a trembling breath.

Hazel brings the tube of light up to my face, and then hesitates. "You know, shining a UV light this close probably isn't very good for your eyes."

I laugh, and she chuckles. There was a time when we made each other laugh regularly, but that was long ago.

"You ready?" she asks.

I clock the fear in her eyes and it gives me a moment's pause. "Yes."

I blink once so that the creature is large in my vision, then, as the bar of ultraviolet light fills my field of view, I close my eyes.

The creature holds fast, going nowhere, reacting exactly as it had with the pen light.

Suddenly a small black hole burns into its body, then another, the holes incinerating matter as they widen. It's like watching film melting in a cine-projector.

I want to say something, to tell the others that it's working, but I'm breathless. The creature's legs curl inward, forming a shriveled ball that continues folding in on itself until, twenty seconds or so after the UV light had first been applied, nothing remains save for a couple of limbs swirling in my vision like floaters.

"Well?" Hazel asks as I open my eyes.

I can't find the words. Instead, my face cracks into a broad grin and suddenly I feel like crying.

"Yeah?" she says.

I nod.

"It worked! Jesus Christ, it worked!"

Milton yells in triumph and punches the air.

Wasting no time, I slide off the table and let Hazel go next, holding the tube of UV light to her eyes until she confirms that the creature is dead. Then it's Milton's turn. In less than a minute, we're all cured.

Milton is so excited that he leaps from the table and runs out of the operating theater. Hazel and I quickly follow, finding him in the lounge, leaping across the sofas in a state of euphoria.

"We did it!" he cries, checking his watch. "And with an hour to spare!"

"Look at us," Hazel says, staring at me with wide eyes. "We're still doing it. Holding our eyes open, refusing to blink."

"This is going to take some getting used to," I say.

Milton is banging on the window glass now. "We did it, you bastards! We did it!" He continues jumping up and down, eyes screwed tightly shut. "We did it! We did it! We did—"

He freezes.

I know instantly that something is terribly wrong.

Milton's face falls. His mouth drops open as if he's about to say something—and his eyeballs explode, coating the lenses of his spectacles in blood and viscera.

Hazel's hands clamp to her mouth but no sound comes out. She stands rooted as Milton crumples to the floor. A gargled scream escapes her throat and she lurches forward, running to him, dropping to her knees over his spasming body.

I can only look on in horror as Milton stops moving.

Hazel is screaming in anguish now. Her head drops into her hands.

Be careful, I want to say. *Don't close your eyes. It's not over.*

Kneeling beside her, I glance at Milton. His blood-coated glasses have slipped, exposing his eye sockets. Unlike the guard or Doctor Roman, there is nothing at all where Milton's eyeballs were except for some bloody mush. Hazel really shouldn't have to see this.

Perhaps thinking the same thing, Hazel climbs to her feet and runs out of the room. I follow her into the corridor.

"What now?" she asks, her watery eyes pleading.

With my mind in the clutches of a dizzying existential vertigo, I realize that I have no reassuring words for her.

"Didn't we do it?" she asks. "What the hell is going on?"

I gather myself. Grab her hands and squeeze tight. "There's only one way to find out."

I close my eyes.

Seeing only darkness on the backs of my eyelids, I let go of one of Hazel's hands and cover my eyes, making it darker still. I concentrate on a single point.

Instantly I see a pinprick of light, dead center. My heart sinks—it's back.

Then, to my horror, I see another dot of light. Then another. And another...

There are half a dozen of them, maybe. Like a constellation of stars imprinted on my sight. And every one of them is rapidly increasing in size.

My eyes snap open.

Hazel's eyes are closed already. She opens them with a gasp. "The radiation," she says, fear mounting on her face. "It didn't kill the parasites..."

"No," I say, finishing her thought. "It caused them to multiply."

CHAPTER 18

Scrabbling around in my pocket, I pull out the pen lights and switch them on. I shine the lights in my eyes and close them.

The blast of illumination shocks the rapidly evolving creatures, their growth halting. Then, with a pulse, the field of stars become larger blobs. They've continued growing, regardless.

Opening my eyes, I throw the pen lights down in disgust. I turn to Hazel but she's not there. Moving farther down the corridor, I find her in the children's play area of the waiting room, kneeling amongst the toys with a small pink teddy bear held tightly to her chest.

"They're immune to the light now," I inform her.

Tears stream down her face. "We're never going to see her again, are we?"

I want to say something to reassure her, but still I have nothing.

Tears well in her eyes.

"Don't, Hazel."

She blinks, letting the tears fall to her cheeks.

"Hazel! What are you doing? You mustn't blink, for Christ's sake!"

"Why not? What does it matter? I'd rather blink myself to death than die at the hands of those bastards."

Dropping into one of the seats around the perimeter of the play area, I force my eyes wide, but they're lazy, having got used to a few minutes of respite, and start stinging immediately.

In the silence I realize that I can hear the hum of the city. It strikes me as quite remarkable—only a street away, life is continuing as normal. People are going about their business blissfully unaware that, within these walls, the end is nigh. "We can't give up, okay? Not yet."

She stares at me with unblinking eyes, nodding her head almost imperceptibly.

"Okay. Come on. What do we know so far?"

Hazel remains silent.

"They're growing, inside our eyes. They expand when we close them."

She sighs. "They're immune to almost anything we throw at them."

"But what do they want?" Rage twists inside me that I don't have the answers. "What's driving them?"

"Hunger," she says. "They crave human brains."

"Like zombies."

Hazel groans and rolls her eyes.

"That's good," I say. "Rolling your eyes is good, it brings moisture."

"Okay. So keep saying stupid crap and I'll be just fine."

"That's true. Without me your eyes would be like shriveled raisins by now."

"See," she says, the suggestion of a smile on her lips. "You're good for something."

"At last. I've found my calling." I hold her gaze. "I still love you, you know."

She nods slowly. "Is that why you changed the ringtone to *The Twilight Zone* for whenever I call?"

"What? It's my favorite TV show ever."

She snorts laughter. I think she knows I'm telling the truth. We lock eyes.

A loud bang makes us jump.

One of the hazmat-suited soldiers is hitting the glass with the butt of his machine gun. He catches my eye and mimes looking at his watch. From the way his eyes crinkle, I think he's smirking beneath his gas mask.

"Son of a bitch."

A few of his colleagues appear from behind him, peering in at us. Clearly they have nothing better to do now that they've executed everyone in the building.

I leap to my feet and close the blinds.

Rage manifests itself as a twitching nerve between my eyes. I glance at the stopwatch and immediately wish I hadn't.

"Stay here," I say. Marching down the corridor, I open the door to the lounge and step through, smarting at the sight of Milton's body on the floor, empty eye sockets exposed behind his glasses. I search through cupboards and drawers, closets and file cabinets. This is where Milton found the eye baths, after all, so maybe there are other things here that can help us.

There has to be *something*. There just has to be. This can't be the end.

Crossing the room, I step over Milton's corpse and once again catch a glimpse of his face.

I stop dead. Take a second look. Unsure of what I'm seeing, I kneel down beside him for a closer examination.

Steeling myself, I remove his glasses. The creatures have been busy—the optic nerves and eye muscles at the back of the sockets have been eaten away, exposing the base of the brain.

I count three bloated critters resting in this mass of tissue. Two of them move sluggishly, nothing at all like the active creatures I see when I close my eyes. Their antennae wriggle, a few legs flicker, but nothing more.

The third bug doesn't seem to be moving at all.

A rush of insight hits me with such force that I lose my balance and struggle to climb to my feet. I burst through the door and hurry back to the waiting area.

Hazel lifts her head from her hands as she hears me approaching.

"Why do zombies eat brains?" I say.

The spark leaves her eyes. "Oh God, enough with the zombies, already."

"Seriously. It's the chemical inside your brain, right? The mood-altering chemical... What is it?"

Hazel thinks for a moment. "Serotonin?"

"Right! That's it! So what if these things are like little zombies? What if they crave serotonin?"

Hazel frowns, her eyes narrowing. "You mean, they're just junkies after their next fix?"

"Precisely. But it's too much for them to handle when they hit the brain. It's not long before they're... engorged."

"Like they've stuffed themselves fit to burst."

"Yeah, exactly."

"So, if we could somehow satisfy their craving before it's too late…"

"Before the pressure gets too much and our eyes explode…"

Hazel's face lights up. "My God…"

We stand there staring at each other for a long moment.

"So how do we do that?" I ask.

Hazel puffs her cheeks out. "I have an idea, but it will take some doing."

"Well, we'd better work fast." I glance at my stopwatch. "We have fifteen minutes until they come through that door."

CHAPTER 19

I throw open the door to the storage room and charge inside, frantically scanning the shelves of plastic trays filled with small medicine boxes and bottles.

"What is it?" I shout. "A vial or something? What does it look like?"

"You won't find it in there," Hazel says, poking her head into the room. "Come on." She disappears.

I follow her out. "They must have liquid serotonin, though, right? I mean, that must be a thing."

She enters the lounge, shielding her eyes from the sight of Milton's body on the floor. "Even if they did, it wouldn't be of a high enough concentration for what we need."

She continues through the next door until we're back in the operating theater. My stomach rolls. This can't be good.

"We'll have to get ours from the source," Hazel says. Her concerned look suggests she can read the fear on my face. "I'd extract it from myself, but it'll be much quicker if I use you."

I eyeball the operating table in the center of the room, skin prickling with terror. "You're not poking around in my brain."

"I don't have to. There are actually higher concentrations of serotonin in the gut."

I stare at her blankly.

"It's why zombies also eat intestines," she says.

I nod, closing the door and locking it. My heart is pounding so hard in my chest cavity that I fear it might break free. I climb onto the operating table and lie down. My breathing is already getting away from me.

Hazel unpacks a syringe, screwing a large needle onto the hub. She lifts my sweater, exposing my belly. "This will hurt," she says, her hands shaking as she brings the needle to my lower abdomen.

"You really need to work on your bedside manner," I say, my voice trembling.

I drop my head back, focusing on the lighting apparatus hanging down from the ceiling.

Oh boy, I wish I could close my eyes.

I wince as a sharp pain stabs at my intestines, and then cry out as I feel a sensation akin to my guts being filtered through a small hole. After the longest few seconds of my life, I look up to see the barrel of the syringe filled with a watery, yellowish liquid. "So you've got it? You've got the serotonin?"

"Well, I've got a syringe full of intestinal fluid. But it contains high concentrations of serotonin."

"Is that going to work?"

"It'll have to. It's the best we've got."

"Can't you, I don't know, purify it or something?"

Hazel removes the needle and switches it for an ultra-thin one. "That would literally take days. Hold still."

The clatter of instruments unsettles me and I turn to see Hazel holding a terrifying metal clamp. "What's that?"

"It's an eye speculum."

"A *what?*"

"Trust me, you'll need it."

"Sweet Jesus."

There's immediate discomfort around the eyelids of my left eye as the instrument is fitted, and then the skin around the eye is pulled back painfully. This causes pressure to build up around my eyeball, making it feel like it's bulging out of my skull. Hazel repeats the process with the other eye.

On the bright side, at least that's solved the blinking issue.

"What now?" I ask, truly dreading the answer.

"Now for the really painful part," she says.

"I was wrong. You've totally perfected that bedside manner."

"Look, I'm not going to lie to you. We have to inject the serotonin directly into the eyeball."

"W—what?"

"It's the only way."

My body jerks, wanting out. I settle myself. *Dear God.*

Better this than dead, Zack said to me earlier. Of the two options, I'm not sure which I'd prefer right now.

My watch beeps. That can only mean one thing—time's up.

"Focus on a point on the ceiling for me," Hazel says. "And whatever you do, don't move your eyes."

I swallow, gripping tight to the sides of the operating table. As the needle hovers into view I'm suddenly aware that I'm close to hyperventilating.

At that moment there's a blast of gunfire. The thud of a distant door being kicked open.

"They're in the ward," Hazel says, panic rising in her voice.

"Let's do this. Now."

My jaw locks, teeth jamming together. I focus on a single speck on a ceiling tile.

The syringe fills my vision, the needle looming closer. I brace myself.

The thump of feet in the hallway. They're coming.

Doesn't matter. Just concentrate.

I hold my breath.

A long moment.

That wasn't so bad. I didn't feel anything.

A lightning bolt of hot pain pierces my skull. Hazel presses down on the plunger. I scream as a laser bolt shoots through my eyeball in a downward trajectory, feeling for all the world like it has penetrated the back of my head, nailing me to the table.

"Easy," Hazel cries out. "Ajay, careful! Jesus!"

The panic in her voice confuses and terrifies me. I'm not even aware that I've moved. "It's okay," I say, my voice sounding anything but.

The door handle rattles.

"They're here," she says. "Oh God, they're here. We're too late!"

"Hazel. Listen to me. Complete the job, okay?"

I hold fast to my point on the ceiling, even though I've now lost the sight in my left eye. Hazel darts around the operating table. I try looking beyond the needle as it looms in my vision.

No! Not again!

A hideous thought surfaces: even if this works, I might never get over the trauma of this moment. Maybe I'll live out the rest of my days in a state of deranged terror.

A thumping at the door. A quick burst of gunfire. They'll be inside the room in a matter of seconds.

Hazel's hand trembles violently. I reach out and grab her wrist, steadying it.

Before I can muster any reassuring words, the needle penetrates my eyeball.

An explosion of pain blots out my sight entirely. It feels as though Hazel has forced her thumbs into my socket and is pressing on my eye.

I gasp for breath, as if drowning. *Just let me die. Let me die. Let me die.*

There's a sudden and immense relief of pressure as Hazel removes the clamps.

"Shut your eyes," she says.

I reach out and grab her hand. She squeezes it tight.

I close my eyes.

There they are, springing into view in the darkness. Half a dozen creatures, their fully extended jaws snapping as they eat. I want to scream but the sound is lodged in my throat. They're expanding at an incredible rate.

Panic encases my heart—*this is it.* The pressure will get too much at any moment.

The bugs are not growing, I suddenly realize. They're bloated.

One of the swollen critters stops eating, its abdomen still expanding, and suddenly it bursts like a pimple. A second bug pops, its gooey innards splatting across my vision, then dispersing. Another creature explodes. Then another...

It's working! I want to cry, but my mouth won't move. The pain has paralyzed me.

"Ajay! What's happening?"

A rattle of gunfire followed by a clang of metal as the door lock is destroyed. The theater door creaks open.

It's around this time that I pass out.

CHAPTER 20

"And they all lived happily ever after." I close the storybook. "The end."

Mia beams as she sits on the bed, surrounded by her favorite cuddly toys. "That was good, wasn't it?"

"Very good. Okay, time for bed." I give her a big hug.

She squeezes me tight. "I love you, too, Daddy."

I chuckle. "I love you too as well."

I stroke her hair. Breathe her in. Something as simple as a cuddle from my daughter now seems like the most amazing thing in the world. Both Hazel and I kept our distance from her for a week after the incident, until we'd been given the all-clear. Mia had lots of sleepovers at Granny's in the meantime.

"Are you and Mummy back together now?" Mia asks, sliding under the bedcovers.

I smile a little uneasily, not sure what to tell her. "We're working on it."

"I love my new room, Daddy," she says.

"Oh, well, in that case, I've got some good news. Mummy said you can stay over more often, okay?"

She cheers. I kiss her on the forehead. "Goodnight, Peanut."

"Night night. Hope the bed bugs bite!"

I scream in mock terror. "I hope they don't!"

Mia laughs.

Exiting the room, I leave the door ajar a little.

Hazel stands in the hallway. "Well," she says. "I'd better be off."

"I guess."

"You've made the place real nice." She grabs her coat.

"Thanks. You can always… you know… stay over."

Hazel smiles apologetically. "You know I can't."

She opens the door and exits onto the public landing.

"I'll drop her off on Sunday night," I say.

She nods, holding the look for a moment, then turns and walks away.

I close the door. Maybe this is my happily ever after. And if it is, then I'll take it. I shudder to think what could have been.

The parasite was reported in the media as the outbreak of a virus, as if it had been nothing more than a stomach bug or a bout of diarrhea. Two-hundred and thirty-eight people are reported to have died, although I suspect the true number to be at least double that. The entire incident has been a PR nightmare for the hospital, which remains closed, most likely never to reopen. The truth as I know it is being kept under wraps, and, quite frankly, that's probably for the best.

No point in all that scaremongering.

I go to my room and prepare for bed. Ever since things returned to normal, I've looked forward to going to sleep at night. It's a real luxury.

I climb into bed and turn out the light. In the darkness the thoughts come, as they always do. I can't help wondering if all the clinical trial patients made it back to the hospital that day, before the lockdown. Or if anyone brushed past me in the busy food court at the motorway service station. How many infected are still out there?

I could drive myself crazy thinking about it.

When eventually I drift off, my mind whisks me into the same nightmare I've been having for the past week. I'm trapped somewhere. The location changes every night—sometimes it's a castle, or a mansion, or a vast skyscraper—but just as I locate the exit, I find myself back at the beginning again. There's no escape.

A sudden scream pierces the bubble of my dream world. It takes a few moments but then, to my horror, I recognize the source.

It's Mia.

I jerk awake, heart jackhammering. I can think only the worst.

It's morning already. A strip of sunlight shines in between the blinds. Mia stands over me.

"Oh, Daddy," she says. "You scared me."

I grab her. Check her over. "What's wrong, Peanut? What is it? Why were you screaming?"

"Because," she says. "You were sleeping with your eyes wide open."

About the Author

SPIKE BLACK writes high concept horror novels and suspense thrillers. His books include *Don't Look Inside* (a 2015 Kindle Book Awards finalist), *Leave This Place*, *Ghost Ahead*, and *Blink Dread*. He is currently working on several volumes of short stories for his *Avert Your Eyes* series.

Bookstore: spikeblack.com/amazon
Website: spikeblack.com
Facebook: spikeblack.com/facebook

SPIKE BLACK'S
GHOST AHEAD

Some mistakes come back to haunt you…

Tortured by his decision to leave the scene of a fatal hit and run, Garth's guilty conscience causes him to see ghostly apparitions of the victim. But when cars identical to his own start crashing at the scene of the accident, Garth discovers that the ghost is real — and it's hunting him down, hell-bent on revenge…

Buy *Ghost Ahead* from Amazon

SPIKE BLACK'S
DON'T LOOK INSIDE

Lizzie finds an old, tattered book and is intrigued by its creepy cover. Suddenly the words DON'T LOOK INSIDE scratch furiously into the leather, as if carved by an invisible hand. Lizzie jolts, terrified. She absolutely intends to heed the warning. No way in *hell* is she opening the book now.

But her curiosity gets the better of her. She feels compelled to look inside. Her hands move with a will of their own, opening the book. The suspense is too much. Her heart hammers in her chest as she reads the first line.

No. She reels in horror. *What have I done?* She should have obeyed the warning. She never should have looked inside. But now it's too late. Because the book knows her darkest secret, and it's about to exact a hideous punishment...

Buy *Don't Look Inside* from Amazon

SPIKE BLACK'S
LEAVE THIS PLACE

Silas wakes with a start in the middle of the night, feeling a suffocating sense of unease - as if he's being watched. His wife is asleep. He scans the bedroom of their rented holiday cottage, a spooky and unfamiliar place.

He makes out something in the dark. On the chair in the corner of the room. *What the…?* He's mistaken, surely. It's his over-active imagination. It's a trick of the moonlight.

No. Something's there. A figure, hunched forward. An old man. The same old man he's seen in a framed photograph on the bedroom wall. Sitting there, watching them sleep. With a terrifying grin on his face…

Buy *Leave This Place* from Amazon

Printed in Great Britain
by Amazon